PALMERS HILL

To all those RAF aircrew who fought in World War Two,
through whose courageous actions we enjoy the freedoms
of our today and to their families who were bereaved.

*The photograph of Mac's Spitfire with its ground crew on the back cover
is reproduced by kind courtesy of Wing Commander Chris Goss.*

PALMERS HILL

— IAN MORRIS —

BREWIN BOOKS

First published by
Brewin Books Ltd, 56 Alcester Road,
Studley, Warwickshire B80 7LG in 2009
www.brewinbooks.com

ISBN: 978-1-85858-459-1

A Cataloguing in Publication Record
for this title is available from the British Library.

Typeset in Bembo
Printed in Great Britain by
Cromwell Press Group

Contents

Acknowledgements

I am grateful for the help and encouragement of many people I have received in writing this book. I am sure that every author singles out particular people with some trepidation but it would be wrong if I did not take the plunge and I hope others will be charitable and not see that in any way as a sleight.

The nephews of Mac and Barry Goodwin have been stalwarts in providing family information and anecdotes which I have woven into the story so tightly that they have said they are no longer sure what is and what is not fiction. But I, the author know! John Birch and his late wife Janet who used to own Palmers Hill and who took such pleasure in sharing their knowledge of it with me. Janet provided the link that enabled me to trace the nephews!

Eric Carter, now approaching his nineties and an intrepid pilot who flew both Spitfires and Hurricanes; the latter in zero temperatures in Russia! Galen Bartholomew who took me through the 'rigours' endured by pupils educated at the famed school, The Wells House at Malvern. Roger Fowler who gave me the 'feel' for hill climbing at Shelsley Walsh. Jim Snell, a retired architect, who was kind enough to research for me how a house of Palmers Hill calibre would have been built in the early 1920s. And finally but by no means least, my wife, Jane, who has had to endure the reading of most of the book to her aloud!

Ian Morris
November 2009

Chapter 1

THE BEGINNING OF THE END

On a cold frosty morning in December 1951 Laughton Goodwin deliberately rose early before the rest of the family. A tall rather gaunt figure of a man now; his head balding with a shock of white hair at each side of his skull to which he religiously applied Brylcreem each morning to smooth it down. A shadow of his former self he was no longer as handsome as he had been when younger. Yet he liked to think that whilst disease and worry had taken its inevitable toll there was something of his old self still there, of the man whose very presence had once commanded attention.

Slowly with difficulty and in obvious pain he left Jessie still deeply asleep in their double bed and went over to the heavy armchair where he had draped his red silk quilted dressing gown the night before. He had bought it at Gieve's & Hawkes on one of their expeditions to London. He pulled it on over his pyjamas and put his feet into his slippers. Even that small action made him wince now. He rested his hands on the back of the chair and quietly sighed before summoning his energy, he moved into the bathroom to shave and clean his teeth. He had always been meticulous about his personal appearance. What had his mother always said when he had complained about cleaning his shoes ready for the last day of term, 'last day as good as the first'. A bitter smile met the memory.

Washing and shaving meant he had to remove his dressing gown and pyjama top and that used up even more of his precious energy. He lathered up with hot water and Coté shaving soap. Now looking at himself in the mirror over the basin he used his Rolls safety razor to remove the stubble of his beard first from the right side and then from the left tensing his cheeks with his fingers as he did so; then around his mouth and from his chin. He washed and dried his razor and shaving brush and put them away. He cleaned his teeth, still his own, with Milk of Magnesia toothpaste and rinsed his mouth.

Mixing hot and cold water to an even temperature in the white porcelain sink, now he washed under his arms, pushing the soapy flannel across his chest and then round to include the back of his neck and ears. Then after passing over his skin once more with a rinsed flannel, he dried himself thoroughly on the soft white towel which was hanging on the heated rail. There, that was enough. Taking a clean pair of pyjamas from the cupboard he put them on, tied the cord round his waist and then donned his dressing gown again. Picking up his towel he folded it and put it back on its rail before leaving the bathroom quietly to listen to the house.

Good, no sign that any one else was stirring. As he had planned, it was much too early on a Sunday morning for any of the remaining family to be awake let alone up. The pain from his now chronic neuritis was even worse this morning than it had been yesterday. It simply would give him no peace.

Stephen Gosling, his good friend and faithful doctor had told him there was no cure. There had been a chance a few years back that he could have surgery but that had been ruled out when the anaesthetist had examined him and declared that he would be at such risk from the halothane anaesthetic that he might not come through the operation.

All that had been three years ago and had made him even more depressed. Stephen had prescribed a drug to help him but he had felt it made him worse and had stopped taking it even before the course was half way through. He had never liked taking tablets anyway and had not bothered Stephen about how he felt after that. His upbringing had made it alien to him to talk about feelings.

He left the bedroom and went towards the stairs. As he did so he passed his daughter's bedroom. Betty now had her husband, Bob Walker, to look after her. He was a good steady chap who with his Scottish husbandry perhaps would curb her spending which he ruefully reflected, her father had singularly failed to do! He paused to look in on his two grandsons whom he adored. There they both were, fast asleep curled up with their respective bears; Mike now nearly six and Tony, three.

Their peaceful tranquillity was something that he envied; his own insomnia had curtailed his sleep for almost the length of Tony's lifetime. He reached the top of the stairs. His destination was the Gun Room at the rear of the house. Slowly he descended the stairs one at a time. He knew every creak that each step could utter and managed to avoid most so as not to risk disturbing those who still slept upstairs. Eventually, after yet more minutes had passed he entered the room and having closed the door he switched on the light.

As he slowly and silently slid back the heavy brocaded curtains one by one and let in the grey light of dawn he could just see that there had been a particularly hard frost. It lay now like white diaphanous muslin draped over the grass lawns that ran down towards the swimming pool. The dark boughs of the nearer trees stood festooned in white hoar, sentinel dark silhouettes before the acres of deciduous woodland that lay beyond.

He sat down at his desk and opening a drawer on the right-hand side extracted various components that he set out on the leather bound surface in front of him.

He turned to his small workbench and taking two new shell cases he slightly swaged their open ends ready to receive the bullets. Next, he fitted each with a new primer and placed them upright on the bench, before filling the cases with a carefully measured quantity of the powder he had made up the previous day. Last, he inserted the bullets and pressed each in turn to seat and crimp them.

He had made just the two rounds he needed. He put them to one side of the desk. They lay there glinting in the light without a hint of their deadly purpose. He struggled to his feet and shuffled to one of the cabinets which were mounted on the wood panelled walls of this elegant room. With a key from a bunch he had also extracted from the desk drawer he unlocked the cabinet and removed his Webley service revolver.

Taking it over to the desk to where the two bullets were, he broke the gun and inserted each shell into two consecutive chambers of the cylinder before closing the two halves of the gun together. A firm metal click sounded on the silence of the room as it locked into place. He picked up the gun and making sure that the safety catch was on placed it in the deep right hand pocket of his dressing gown.

There was no more time. People would soon be waking. Picking up his ebony walking stick with the silver engraved handle, the one Jessie had given him when he broke his leg in that fall from his hunter two decades before, Laughton eased his way towards the door and opened it again quietly and listened for sounds from upstairs. There were none. Painfully slowly he made his way along the corridor that led to the back hall. Its walls were lined with trophies of hunting days in Scotland when he was young and fit; able to lead his life to the full. Now he shuffled past with no hope of a future. Quietly he opened the tradesmen's door into the yard at the rear and made his way outside into the garden.

A few minutes passed step upon step until he reached the glade where he had so often sat on sultry still summer evenings enjoying a pipe or playing with the children as they had grown up. The bench over there was where he wanted to be. He had cut the timbers for it himself. He had made it working with his sons when they were just teenagers. The bench was like him now, old and brittle but it would still take his weight.

As at last he sat down he flicked off the safety catch and pointing the gun into the bank he pulled the trigger. It fired instantly. The gun was in perfect working order then! At last in the acres of deciduous woodland that surrounded his home in the burgeoning light of a cold dawn a multitude of thoughts raced through his mind.

His own voice and recollection were predominant. Accompanying and embellishing his own were other voices and vivid moments from the past, come as if to share his last moments; to speak within him; through him; disjointed memories of the past sixty eight years flooding his mind. Some of the voices he recognised instantly; some he identified from events re-lived; some spoke of things about which he had no prior knowledge. The past and the present suddenly, somehow, were flowing into each other's streams as if his life with the lives of his children were running waters which had become a vast river into whose secrets he was admitted in remembrance present.

And amidst it all, it seemed as if his two boys were there with him seated in his mind as they had sat with him as youngsters on this very bench those many years before when he had answered their simplistic questions. All those questions that Jessie and he had asked themselves for so many years perhaps now would be answered.

Chapter 2

THE EARLY YEARS

Few recollections of his early years came to mind. He remembered little of his life as a child at the back end of the last century save a wispy visual picture of his father, Tom. His father he recalled had always seemed a distant figure. A tall slim man he had possessed pitch black hair with full sideburns which made him look frighteningly severe. Despite that forbidding appearance Laughton could never remember his father demonstrating any unkindness to him or his brothers and sister even if his appearance might have suggested otherwise.

Tom he recalled had seen little by way of formal education and had been born to a life dominated by hard physical work. The fear of ending his days in the Poor House had driven him to possess an almost paranoid desire to seek a better existence. Like his father before him he had trained to be a miller to work in the family firm based in Dudley. The firm, of which his father eventually became head following the death of his grandfather, had in fact had been reasonably profitable even in his father's early years there, save when there had been downturns in the market. The ironic reality as it seemed to Laughton seeing it now was that his father had never really been in danger of being impecunious although his recollection was of marked frugality at home until the merger that had brought a promise of riches beyond his father's expectations.

He recalled the excitement when he was about ten that surrounded that event. His father had come home early and he had overheard him telling his mother that the family's fortunes would now be assured. There was to be an amalgamation of Goodwin's Extra Flour with Fosters who were canned food importers and a provision merchant called Brown. The new firm was going to be called Goodwin, Foster and Brown. At last, his father had told his mother they would be able to exploit the gap he had identified in the brewing market for yeast. The evening stood out in Laughton's memory. It was one of the few occasions that he recalled his father having had too much to drink and of him smiling inanely in his cups.

The family had lived at that time in a house on the outskirts of Dudley. He could recall little detail about the house now save its atmosphere. It had always felt homely but perhaps that was not so much the house and its mid-Victorian architecture but because of his mother's input. Esther had been a Grainger before she had married his father. The Grainger family had made their mark in Worcester producing 'blue' porcelain. It was even said that one of her forbears had immigrated to America and started a china factory there in a place that later had taken his name as 'Graingerville'. Whether that was true he had never discovered but it was part of the family folklore.

Esther's family had been quite a bit wealthier than the Goodwins and her parents had been furious when Tom had come to claim her hand. She had told Laughton that they had told her that she would be cut off from any of the family monies if she married Tom. She had with the impetuosity of youth ignored the threat and married Tom. Her family had been true to its word. His parents had never seen any of the Grainger wealth! No doubt that had fed his father's paranoia.

He remembered his mother as small and quite petite with brown gentle eyes that always seemed full of patient love for the many children she had borne his father. Two of his siblings he had never known. They had died in their infancy just months old as so many infants did in those days. His mother had been a most capable woman and well suited to the busy life of bringing up his sister Connie and his five brothers. He and his brothers especially had adored her. She was a true matriarch and when she had eventually died it was as if a huge light had been extinguished in his life.

Her gentle hands had nurtured him and cared for each of them as if she had no pressure of time upon her. When Laughton was fourteen, he had left school and had begun to serve his apprenticeship in the family firm. He had recognised fairly early on that he was not as bright as his younger brother. Stanley had won a scholarship at the local grammar school and continued his education eventually gaining a place at Birmingham University. Their intellectual differences had not mattered then although perhaps later they had contributed to their difficulties. Their relationship when young had always been a particularly close and special one.

It was with Stanley that he recalled first playing cricket with a hard ball and breaking his first window! He must have been about seven. They had continued to play cricket together throughout their teens and had managed regular places playing for the local Blakedown eleven.

There they had played with Fred Jackson who went on to play for Worcestershire. It was through that chance that Connie had met Fred and later they had married. Thinking of Fred, he recalled how they had both enjoyed shooting and fishing together. Fred was a good shot but in competition always rather nervous. Unlike Laughton himself, he had not made it to Bisley! Laughton recalled how proud he had been to have finished so high up in the rankings all those years ago. Of such little importance now in the scheme of things!

Three years before he had met Jessie after Stanley was back from college with his degree in engineering, he and Stanley had decided to set up in business together. Laughton had finished his apprenticeship in 1899. Milling flour and the production of yeast were not activities which had attracted him at all. He saw the emergence of the motor car as having better business opportunities and challenge for him. He had been studying automobile engineering in his spare time. He had found that Stanley was easily persuaded to his way of thinking.

At his father's suggestion they had gone together and seen a wealthy family friend, Sir Jim Smith, who lived at Whitley Court. What a place that was in those days. The magnificent fountain splaying water high up into the air and all those rooms! What must have the owner thought about these two ambitious young men who wanted to set up a garage he could not imagine now. Nevertheless it was Sir Jim Smith who had been willing to put up fifty percent of the money they needed to make a start.

They had started as they had planned in a small way by renting a workshop in New Road, Kidderminster. Those premises undoubtedly had room for expansion if they got that far. Their father had put up some more of the money which was required and a loan from the bank had supplied the balance.

He recalled the day when he and Stanley had erected the new sign. 'Castle Motor Company' it said in big red letters on a stark yellow background. He winced now at the memory of its garishness and involuntarily smiled. They had been so proud of it at the time. Fortunately, later their taste had changed and become more sophisticated.

They both worked hard and had recruited and trained employees who also were fired with the idea that the automobile was here to stay. The business soon thrived as more and more cars and vehicles were being produced for the road. They sold cars and repaired them. People trusted them and thought their service was the best in the area.

They were even able to start their own apprenticeship scheme. They formed a limited company and he had become its first managing director. If only they had possessed the extra money then to develop their own car. Whilst Stanley had by then designed a three wheeler, which he called a 'cycle car' they had not had sufficient funds to build even a prototype.

In their usual way they had tried. They had asked Sir Jim Smith to put up some more money but he had told them there was too much risk involved in being a small motor manufacturer and in any event he would not think of considering it until they had paid off his existing loan! They had not bothered to ask their father or the bank anticipating similar dusty answers!

Chapter 3

JESSIE

He had met Jessie in the summer of 1910. He was twenty six. It had been on one of those sunny cricket days when he had been playing against the Chaddesley Corbett village side. The first thing he recalled about her was her laughter. She was in what they termed the club house with a group of other women from the local side preparing the tea. He recalled she was cutting bread with a long carver from large loaves for one of the other women to spread.

He was putting his pads on getting ready to go in to bat. When he had heard her laughing he had turned and looked in her direction. His first impression was that she was slim with cascading black hair which somehow seemed to dance around her pretty face as she moved. Their eyes had somehow met at that moment and she had briefly smiled at him before looking back to her task. There had been an instant attraction for him in that smile. Then applause had broken through his thoughts as he had done up the last clasp on his pad. The number three whose name he could not now remember had just been bowled out. As he walked to the crease his mind still lingered on the owner of that smile.

He had then played well and in the total of a hundred and fifty runs which had won the match that July day he had scored nearly forty-five including the winning run! It had been one of his best innings. When his team had come in for tea afterwards he looked around to try and find the girl who had smiled at him but she was not there.

He was disappointed. He made what he hoped would sound an idle enquiry of one of the older women who was pouring tea out of a large heavy-looking, brown enamel teapot holding its handles with both hands. His brief description had brought the immediate recognition 'Oh I think you mean Jessie Palethorpe do you?' He had asked where Jessie lived as he needed to get in touch with her. The woman had smiled knowingly at him and he recalled blushing.

'Up at the Hall, you know Brockencote Hall?'

'Her father is the man who makes the sausages,' she added. She had pointed the spout meaningfully in the direction of the cold sausages which formed just part of the generous tea buffet. Surely, he had thought, the wooden table spread with its immaculate white linen cloth could not be safe with the weight it bore of such a generous tea; sausages together with plate upon plate of egg, ham and salmon sandwiches; not to mention the different varieties of cake! He helped himself to a white china plate onto which he collected some salmon sandwiches and went off to eat them leaving the woman to carry on pouring tea.

Chapter 4

THE PALETHORPES

He knew the Hall. He had heard of the Palethorpes. The Palethorpes had a large fleet of vans that used to deliver throughout the Midlands from their factory in Tipton. Occasionally one of them would break down in Kidderminster and he or Stanley would send out for it to be recovered and repaired at the garage.

'Charles Henry' as he was known must be the girl's father. He had met him just once or twice when he had been up at the Brinton factory discussing some engineering problem with Cecil and 'Charles Henry' had been there. He was a formidable businessman and had really built up the Palethorpe sausage enterprise in the last few years. He had recently heard that they now had their own railway siding so that the sausages could be despatched to the Dominions!

He had not seen Jessie again for a few months. Then quite by chance he was over at Chaddesley Corbett visiting a potential customer. With hindsight he congratulated himself that he had been wearing a grey pin-striped suit instead of his usual blue overalls.

He was in the butcher's shop buying some steak for his supper when she had come in. She was wearing a pale blue dress that set off her hour glass figure to perfection. He had instantly recognised her. She had smiled at him with obvious recognition.

'Don't I know you from the cricket?' she confidently ventured. 'But I'm sorry I don't think I know your name.'

'Goodwin ...... Laughton Goodwin' he had rather stumblingly replied 'and yours is Jessie Palethorpe isn't it?' he had added as his confidence increased.

'Yes ...... yes it is. How very nice to meet you Mr. Goodwin,' she had said putting what seemed a slight emphasis on the word 'very'. He had finished his purchase and waited whilst she was served. As they had made their way out of the shop he had engaged her again in conversation. Neither had hurried to leave the other and eventually just before he recognised that she was ending the conversation he had summoned up the courage to ask her if they could meet again.

Her answer was to invite him for tea at the Hall that Thursday. They had agreed a time of four o'clock. He drove back to Kidderminster in a euphoric state and had rushed in to tell Stanley of his good fortune when he had arrived back.

The following Thursday he had taken special care with his appearance. He had shaved until his cheeks almost shone. He wore his grey velvet jacket and flannel trousers. His black shoes gleamed. From the garage in Kidderminster he had driven his recently acquired black Wolseley and arrived in Chaddesley Corbett well in advance of the time she had bidden him.

He drove past the entrance drive leading up to Brockencote Hall and turned left into the village. Stopping the car he opened the face of his hunter watch. It was still only a quarter to four. He parked adjacent to the church and locked the car before sauntering up to the lych-gate. A notice to one side announced that this was St Cassian's. How many coffins he idly wondered had this gate protected in past centuries? In a sense of curiosity he was drawn into the churchyard patterned with graves of every previous age. He was struck by the silent quiet of it all. 'What a wonderful place to be laid to rest in' he thought to himself as he opened the door to the church and breathed in the stillness that lay inside. Almost as the thought passed through his mind he had remembered the real purpose of the day; realised he was nearly late and rather flustered by his odd oversight he had hurried quickly to the car and driven back to Brockencote Hall.

It was a beautiful day now that the sun had come out and as he had turned into the long straight drive light dappled light through the thick leaved trees that lined his path. At the end passing a lake on the right the Hall was revealed in all its Victorian splendour. Was that a tower at the end? There was ample room to park.

He was received at the massive oaken front door by a uniformed man, whom he had taken to be the butler. He had been welcomed most courteously. He was obviously expected and was shown into a large drawing room full of the sunshine of the day overlooking an expanse of fields where sheep were trying to graze on bone dry grassland beyond a ha-ha. He had been left for a few moments alone during which he had taken in his surroundings.

The luxury of the damask covered sofas and the fine antiques including the beautiful oil paintings that adorned the walls spoke of the wealth of the Hall's owner. He felt rather overwhelmed. Being rich was so relative. His own family was now financially secure and far from poor but this was something else besides. His reverie was interrupted by hearing chatter from the hallway and her laugh as she had vibrantly entered the room with her mother. 'Hello' she had simply said by way of friendly greeting and then turning to her mother 'this is Mr Laughton Goodwin mother.'

Her mother came forward and had held out her hand in greeting for him to take. 'Come and sit down Mr Goodwin and we will have some tea. May we call you Laughton?' Her easy manner dispersed most of his apprehension.

'Please do' he replied.

The mother was quite short and rather overweight. She was dressed in dark unfashionable clothes but he noticed that her eyes sparkled brightly and she seemed quite friendly. She spoke to the butler who had followed them in.

'Archie please will you bring in the tea for us.'

Mother took charge of the conversation until she had explored his background but by the time tea appeared she seemed content that his intentions were beyond reproach at least for the time being! She excused herself saying 'I have much to do so I will leave you two young people alone for bit. No please do not feel the need to stand!' she hastily added as she rose to go causing him to leap to his feet. Nonetheless he courteously stood as she smiled at him and her daughter before sweeping out of the room. As he sat down again Jessie said, 'Oh don't mind Mother she just likes to check up on me. Now tell me when can we go out together but it will have to be in a foursome!?'

He had been quite taken aback by this rather forthright approach from this confident young woman. He had however with quick thinking remembered that the time for the annual Albrighton Woodland Hunt Ball was near. He knew that would be an attractive invite to most girls. She accepted with alacrity and that turned out to be their first real date.

In his white tie and tails he had driven her home late that night after dropping off his friend Arthur and that rather dippy girl he was taking out. He had seen Jessie in her white silk ball gown to the front porch. She really was a beautiful young woman. How he had enjoyed the fun they had had on their first date dancing together. She was a consummate ballroom dancer but had not embarrassed his lack of ability rather preferring to help him.

Before she could ring for the butler to admit her he had taken a chance and leant forward intending to plant a 'goodnight' kiss demurely on her cheek. How amazed and delighted he was when she had pulled him to her and kissed him with vigour on his lips. He had been kissed by other girlfriends in the past but not on their first date neither with such enthusiasm! He had always remembered that first touch of her lips, the soft perfume of her as he had held her in his arms and how he had driven home thinking that something very special had happened that night. It was only later that he had appreciated that at that moment he had fallen deeply in love with Jessie.

By the standards of that time theirs had been a relatively short courtship he thought. He became a frequent visitor to the Hall. He remembered those times as some of his happiest but was that just because he was looking back to his salad days when every experience was fresh and new?

Chapter 5

ENGAGED AND MARRIED

It was not until the winter of 1912 when there was snow on the ground and Jessie and he had gone out to celebrate his twenty-ninth birthday that he actually felt able to propose to her. Castle Motors now with a small but significant workforce was going well and he was Managing Director. He was earning enough money to be able to purchase a house and to keep himself and a wife.

He had longed for this moment. Earlier in the week he had visited Nathans, the jewellers, in Corporation Street, Birmingham. The night before he did so he had managed to inveigle Jessie into letting him look closely at a ring that had been her maternal grandma's, a pretty pearl set in a gold band. Whilst she went to get her handbag before they went out and he was left alone he had quickly put the ring on a receipt which happened to be in his pocket and drawn round it outside and in with his silver propelling pencil. Armed with those dimensions he had chosen their engagement ring. He had thought that the man from Nathans was most helpful and attentive. He had shown him a wide selection of rings and pointed out that the diamond rings were much in fashion. Laughton was not a fool. He noticed that they were also the most expensive! But nonetheless he had found one with three matching diamonds in a straight row that he particularly thought Jessie would like. His heart had ruled his head and he had thrown financial caution to the winds and bought it!

Now they had enjoyed dinner together and he had taken her back to Brockencote Hall. Those days he usually went in with her for a while after they had been out. They were able to use the snug to be together whilst they had coffee or a sandwich if they had been to the theatre. Sometimes Jessie would play the Broadwood baby grand piano that was in that room. Her father had bought it for her when she was a child. Its satin rosewood finish had been lovingly polished and had a deep patina. More important it appeared to have a glorious tone to one who like Laughton knew little about music. He particularly liked it when she played Beethoven's *Fur Elise* for him. The piece rapidly became his favourite of that time. Jessie's parents never embarrassed them by coming in so as their relationship became more intimate they were able to kiss and pet without having to worry.

Tonight he sat Jessie down in her usual place at the end of the cream brocade sofa which faced the white marble fireplace. He stooped down and kissed her before kneeling down in front of her. Instead of the carefully worded speech he had prepared as he was shaving before coming out he suddenly found himself nervous and speaking rather fast.

'Jessie .... you know how I feel about you, will you marry me?' The words blurted out. He produced the ring box and opened it so she could see the ring inside in its dazzling brilliance as it caught the light of the room as if her reply somehow rested upon it.

'Oh Laughton how lovely ...... but aren't you going to tell me?'

'Tell you what?' he replied wracking his brains, fearful that his proposal was inadequate in some way.

'Tell me you love me, silly!' Jessie had answered smiling at him at his apparent embarrassment.

'Oh that ...... yes of course I do my dear.'

'Then the answer is 'yes' my dear.'

She rose and taking his free hand she helped him up. As they stood together facing each other he took the ring from its box as she held it. She held out her left ring finger. He slipped the ring on. It fitted perfectly. Aglow with smiles she was in his arms kissing him and hugging him with tears of happiness in her eyes. It had been a magical moment.

Not so magical had been him seeking permission for them to be married from Jessie's father, Charles Henry. It was almost a week after Jessie had accepted him that he had summoned up the courage. Jessie had already broken the news to her mother who was on their side but had promised not to say a word to Charles Henry. So Laughton had arrived as was his wont at the Hall at about six o'clock but not on this occasion to collect Jessie and take her out for the evening.

It was a Thursday and he had been forewarned that Charles Henry would be in. When he knocked Archie answered the door and Jessie had appeared behind him. Once the butler had gone they exchanged a quick kiss and Jessie told him he would find her father alone in the drawing room. Then with a smile and another blown kiss she had disappeared into the back of the house.

He knocked and hearing the one word 'come' he had gone into the drawing room. Charles Henry was sorting through some books that were in a pile by the side of his armchair. He stood up when Laughton entered and had met him with a neutral smile.

'How are you Laughton?'

'Well sir, well indeed, and you?'

'Oh I'm fine thank you. I think Jessie is in the snug with her mother if you are looking for her.'

There was a pause and Charles Henry looked at him with what had appeared to Laughton a slightly querulous expression.

'I've actually come to talk to you sir, if it is convenient.'

Suddenly Laughton had hoped it was not and he could be released from this situation that did not seem to be developing as he had anticipated.

'Oh perfectly what can I do for you?'

It was now or never. Laughton realised he could not escape and he rushed into his answer.

'Jessie and I would like to marry and I have come to seek your permission sir.'

'That's a big step Laughton ....' Charles Henry looked at him seemingly very serious and frowned. Laughton's heart missed a beat expecting that he was going to be asked all sorts of questions about his prospects and finances. He could feel sweat rising at his armpits.

Then all of a sudden Charles Henry broke into gales of laughter and coming forward to him had clasped his hand between his own.

'Laughton I am honoured that you have had the courtesy of asking. Both of you are of an age to make up your own minds! Of course you have my permission and my congratulations. Well matched, well matched, that you are! Did you really think that I didn't know why you were here? Come on lets get the family in and we will have a glass on it!'

Laughton almost sighed with relief. The old man had a reputation for being obstinate and difficult. But this time he had been teasing him all along!

They were married on 12th July the following year at the Church of the Redeemer. It was a Baptist ceremony as Jessie and her family were confirmed Baptists. Laughton never had had much attachment to any church or faith. He had been brought up a Christian. Indeed his family had possessed their own pew in their local church but most of it had washed over him and he was not sure now whether he really believed in the existence of a God especially a benevolent one. Nevertheless Jessie had been enthusiastic about a church wedding and he had not demurred. She could have asked for a wedding on the moon and had he been able to acquire it for her he would have done so!

The actual day was cloudy with sunny intervals, typical English summer weather. They were surrounded by friends and family in droves. Jessie wore traditional white, a long organza train borne up by numerous child relatives acting as bridesmaids. When he turned to see her coming up the aisle on the arm of Charles Henry he was stunned by her radiance. The rest of the service, indeed the day passed in a bit of a daze and frankly he had few memories of it.

Lying in her arms much later after making love to her for the first time on their honeymoon in the Cotswolds it had all seemed a bit of a dream.

Chapter 6

THE BIRTH OF THE 'BOYS'

They had bought "The Cottage" in Hagley before the wedding. He had been obliged to borrow money on a mortgage to pay for its purchase and also to have some work done before they could inhabit it. The rooms were small but it had been a cosy home once renovated. Jessie had chosen light colours for the walls and woodwork. He had been allowed to choose the carpets. He had acquired them at wholesale prices through his acquaintanceship with Cecil Brinton whose company Brintons produced very fine carpets in Kidderminster. Whilst he could remember that they had all been woven in pure wool he could now only visualise the stair carpet had been heavily patterned and warm in colour.

The refurbishments had been completed by the end of their week's honeymoon. When they moved in, he being rather a romantic at heart had opened the newly painted outside door with its brass knocker and surprised Jessie by picking her up bodily and carrying her over the threshold. She had been feather light in those early days. Their relationship had been so close. Often they had found comfort and joy in making passionate love in each other's arms, something that was sadly just a faint memory now. Once established in their new home he recalled how they had so enjoyed those first few weeks of having their own home to themselves and finding places for things to be kept.

It was there the following April that early one morning he had heard retching sounds from the bathroom next to their bedroom. Going to investigate he had found Jessie with her head over the lavatory being sick.

'Are you all right?' he asked when clearly she wasn't. She stopped retching and let him help her back to bed. She looked ghastly pale. He was worried that something had badly disagreed with her. He was completely bowled over when she said.

'Laughton I think I am pregnant! I missed last month and now this!'

He had been unsure how he should receive this uncertain news. A moment's thought though had produced gladness. He sat on their bed and put his arm around her and held her. She rested her sick head on his chest and he gently stroked her hair.

'If you are right my dear that will be fantastic news.'

She had been right. About all sorts of things across the years she had been right and he had been wrong.

Her sickness left her after those first weeks and her pregnancy had proceeded unmarred by further difficulties. Her abdomen swelled and there was the time when even he had been able to feel the foetus inside kicking at the wall of her womb. Their happiness that summer at the expectation of birth in December was muted only by the news from abroad which had seemed to be building to an almost inevitable conflict.

When he looked back now war had been a long time coming. The Kaiser seemed intent on spreading German influence and he had always feared that would lead to a war. German industrial power had become a threat to British supremacy in so many areas of the world. Back in the first years of the century the Germans had been building a navy that equalled the British navy in firepower. Meanwhile the nations seemed to have got themselves into two armed camps, each hostile to the other. What was it he had read in the Times about the growth of Serbia and Russia encouraging Serbian citizens to break away from their allegiance to the old Austrian Empire? He couldn't remember now.

He did remember though that when in late June the heir to the Austrian crown was murdered, troops had been sent into Serbia by Austria to find the murderers. Somehow that had seemed to trigger all sorts of diplomatic ties as the winds of war spread wild flames across Europe eventually engulfing Britain and Germany in the conflagration.

Stanley was full of it at work. He did not have a pregnant wife and was much more interested in politics than him. Unlike Laughton he was also excited by the prospect of war. As Kitchener posters went up so many young men seemed to share Stanley's view as they flocked to join up. It was not a view he shared and so he was careful in expressing a view about the hostilities at that time.

As the autumn leaves began to fall and the dew became heavier both he and Stanley had wondered in their own way how the war would affect them. They were both of an age when they might well have to fight. About that they had talked at length! Both of them had been in the Army cadet force when at school and he had always shown a talent for shooting. At least they knew one end of a gun from the other!

Neither had recognised the opportunity that was about to overtake their anxieties. Then they had had a visit from that senior civil servant, Michael Lumley, from London. Their engineering expertise and the capacity of the Castle Motor premises was needed to help make munitions on a scale that would challenge their engineering talents and work their workforce hard until the conflict came to an end. Their organisation and personal direction at their Kidderminster works would be essential to the war effort. They would be not be conscripted.

Of course, there had been no real alternative but to gratefully accept despite Stanley's initial reluctance. Soon engineering drawings for gun parts and shells were reaching them as the British industrial might geared itself up for war. New employees were taken on by the score. He and Stanley were working very long hours to ensure that full production could be met in the shortest time but they had doubted that they could achieve that which was expected of them much before the spring of the following year.

The profit on the pieces they were to produce had been tailored by the War Office's civil servants. On paper they all looked pretty modest. Nevertheless they realised that utilising their business skills, production of the numbers required and more was easily within their grasp. Gradually they had managed to turn 'modest' into 'generous'. Even so they were so concentrating on the challenges set before them that it only slowly began to dawn that if the war went on for any length of time they would both emerge rich men at its end. If they won! They had redoubled their effort.

Then on 23rd December four months into it all, Jessie had gone into a short labour during the morning at home and with the local midwife in attendance she had given birth to a 7lb 4oz boy. He had not been present at the birth but called from a meeting had arrived home soon afterwards. After some heart searching they had decided to call him Henry Macdonald but well before he was out of nappies he had become 'Mac'. He recalled how proud he had been of his newborn child and his thought that the Goodwin line would now be protected for the next generation. At least Mac would not have to fight in a war into which so many nations were now being drawn.

In months it had become almost total war in Europe as the combatant nations grew still more numerous. He and Jessie had talked and had decided to wait a while and have another child after the War had ended. They had not wanted just a single child both having had experience of sharing and the rough and tumble with brothers and sisters when growing up.

The War dragged on. Any hope there was that it would be over quickly had soon been dashed. Stalemate had been rapidly reached on the Western Front in France although that did not stop the appalling losses of life. As he read of that hideous waste of talent rather than feeling fortunate to be in a reserved occupation he had felt guilty that he was not in France doing his bit. The toll of Worcestershire soldiers killed increased. Reading the Kidderminster Shuttle, their local paper, he had found himself drawn to the obituaries where almost daily he recognised the names of young men not much younger than himself who he had known in and around Kidderminster, through school, through work or cricket. One he had recognised as a lad he had himself employed at Castle Motors before he had volunteered. Sometimes as he walked in the street he felt that bereaved parents of young men, whom he had known, recognised him and although polite to him, nevertheless resented his safety.

Far worse for him personally was the return of local soldiers from the Front in France, unable to continue the fight. Some had lost limbs blown off by enemy shells which had landed near them and left many of their mates dead. Others had lost their eyesight in hideous green gas attacks and would be permanently blind. He had noticed them all. Healthy young men no longer whole, with crutches trying to hobble along; or with white sticks tapping their way through familiar streets where old acquaintances crossed roads rather than face the difficulty of finding the right words.

He too had found himself totally unable to face these lambs who had returned abandoned heroes. His abject failure had left him feeling all the more guilt. He had felt so ashamed of himself. Had it been because he had been taking part in making guns and shells that ultimately killed human beings? He had tried to bridge the moral ravine that had seemed to contain his guilt.

Had he not told himself that the nation, his nation, needed the arms which he was helping to manufacture and that those weapons killed the Boche not Tommies! Yet nothing had taken away the guilt that he had felt when faced with the bereaved and the wounded. He had found himself unable even to talk to Jessie about how he felt. It was the first time he had not been able to confide in her.

As the number of volunteers rapidly reduced and conscription took its place the male workforce at Castle Motors had been decimated. Much more frequently now he had to make calls to the War Office in order to plead to keep a man who played a key role in the manufacture of the armaments which they produced.

Stanley and he had become more and more concerned that they would not be able to keep production at its optimum level. They had introduced a shift system to enable the factory to work longer hours without shutting down the machines. They had started to employ women to do the more repetitive tasks. He remembered the time when the women had approached them and asked whether they could do more of the skilled work.

Both Stanley and he had initially fought against having women in the workforce at all and now these women not only wanted to be employed but also on skilled work! It went against all nature. Their place was surely at home bringing up their children. But Stanley and he both knew that they would not be able to continue production at the rate the War Office was dictating unless they did. Caught on the horns of that particular dilemma their principle had not been able to survive the times.

Stanley had been obliged to teach some of them to operate lathes and capstans. He had become an excellent teacher and showed all of them patience

19

beyond anything Laughton would have been able to muster. What had so surprised them both was that many of the women were very adept with the machines and frequently better than the men! The world was fast changing and he had realised that they needed to change with it or fail!

The profit margin on all the government work as they had anticipated improved with time as their production became more efficient. Meanwhile, fortunately the repair work on vehicles needed for the war effort brought in good money. He had watched their fortunes grow as government money flowed into the business. At first he and Stanley had invested all the profits in new plant and machinery but as time went by they had paid off all their loans and their lifestyles became more affluent. Still they worked long hours. Still he had periods when he felt he should be in France. But those periods eventually had receded with him reminding himself that without his skills and those of men like him the war would never be won. Looking back now he recalled those reminders had become less frequent as the months of conflict passed into years and he wondered whether affluence had eventually assuaged his earlier guilt. He suspected that it had and that thought caused him pain.

And then nearly two years into the war Jessie was unexpectedly pregnant again. Her pregnancy this time she wore without effort save a burgeoning bulk. In fact she was as happy as he had ever known her. Mac was coming up two and into mischief at most turns. He was a bonny looking child who had been a bit late walking but after that it had taken all Jessie's time to keep up with him he was so very active. Now there was to be a brother or sister for him. He remembered his own upbringing with his many brothers and Connie and thought how good for Mac to have such a companion.

He smiled a wry smile as he thought of that night when they had come home together from a charity dance. They had enjoyed the evening enormously and on reflection he was sure they had both had quite a bit of alcohol to drink. Anyway, their normal caution had been thrown to the winds. They had made love with sweet abandonment without any precaution. Now there would be another young child in the household. Hopefully, even if it was another boy neither of his sons would have to fight in a war. People were already saying this was turning into a war that would surely end all wars.

The months passed and on 23rd February 1917 Jessie's waters had broken in the early hours and her labour pains had started quite gently at first. It had happened on a night when Mac was fortunately staying with his young Auntie Amy, Jessie's sister who was about to marry Laughton's brother, Bernard. She had always managed Mac so very well. Jessie's contractions were more painful and coming faster as dawn approached and he had been forced to leave her briefly to fetch the midwife, Mrs. Beale, who was only a pace away just down the lane.

By 6am the redoubtable Mrs Beale was back at 'The Cottage' and in charge. He recalled his feelings of relief as he watched her professional ease as she made Jessie more comfortable. By that time Jessie's contractions were less than a minute apart. She was screaming with the pain when the waves hit her. Despite the fact he was mopping her brow with a cold flannel she was still sweating heavily and digging her nails deep into the palm of his hand as he tried to hold her.

He himself had no idea what to do in such a situation but was happy just to busy himself doing things to Mrs. Beale's order. She soon ushered him from the bedroom but he could still hear Jessie's screams until chloroform deadened her pain. Then suddenly he heard a baby's cry and unable to restrain himself any longer from being with her, he rushed upstairs and burst into the bedroom. Mrs Beale glanced up with a frown. She was wrapping a tiny baby with wisps of wet blonde hair in one of the bath towels he had found her from the airing cupboard.

'Congratulations! It's a boy,' she announced, he thought rather unenthusiastically as she passed the small bundle to Jessie whose weary face was now wreathed in smiles. As Laughton had taken Jessie's hand and bent down to kiss her and his new born son he felt ecstatic. Smiling back at Mrs. Beale he had retorted with a laugh,

'Not just a boy Mrs. Beale, but a Barry!' and Jessie had simply kissed the baby lying in her arms and quietly smiled as her lips read 'yes'. They had decided on 'names' sometime before as they had walked on the Clent Hills in waning afternoon sunshine, the previous Autumn; Betty for a girl and Barry for a boy. Guiltily he looked back. He had really hoped for a daughter but recalled thinking at the time that a Betty if that were possible would have to wait until after the war!

Chapter 7

THE CASTLE THREE

The War had finally come to an end. The contracts from the War Office had rapidly ended too after the Armistice. Stanley and he were back to selling and repairing cars. Yet they had expanded the factory throughout the War and they had far more skilled workers and capacity than they now needed. They had discussed reducing their workforce. At some point Stanley had resurrected the idea of them building the three wheeler car that he had designed all those years before. Laughton himself, had by then virtually forgotten about it! He recalled having been rather excited by the prospect encouraged, of course, by Stanley's enthusiasm. At last they had the money, the premises and the skilled workforce to consider such a project.

It had taken a bit of time for Stanley to find the design sketches he had put together. They had spent several evenings meeting at each other's homes carefully examining as to how such a vehicle could be engineered. With their greater knowledge and experience gained in the War they were able to see immediately that it was all perfectly feasible if only they could now find the right engine.

It had been left to him to make enquiries and eventually he had found what he thought was a suitable four cylinder water-cooled engine made by Dorman up in Stafford. It had a 62mm bore and 100mm stroke giving a cubic capacity of 1,207cc. After he had had briefed Stanley about it they had gone to Stafford and examined the engine in detail. Both of them had concluded that it all looked pretty straightforward engineering.

Straightaway they had decided that they could manufacture this engine working with local firms they had used during the War. They could get all the metal forgings and even the cast iron head and separate block manufactured themselves by Alpha Metals at Cradley Heath. They could easily cope with all the machining at their own works including that needed for the connecting rods, the heavy crankshaft and the one-piece cam shaft. They had looked at one or two other engines as 'possibles' but Stanley had chosen the Dorman as being the easiest to produce themselves and the best to use in the three wheeler 'cycle' car he had designed. But their plan could only go ahead if they could get Dorman to let them have a licence to do so.

Some tough and arduous negotiations with the Dorman directors had followed. Several weeks went by before they had managed to persuade them to let the Castle Motor Company manufacture the engine under licence. They had been over the moon at their success. At a single stroke they had not only avoided laying off any of the existing skilled workmen they employed who were 'family' to them but also they had circumvented the considerable costs of getting the complete engines transported from Stafford to Kidderminster. All the parts could be delivered easily by rail from Cradley Heath. No contract with Dorman had been signed at that stage. They felt they needed to produce a couple of prototypes first to see that the whole car would fit together and be saleable.

It must have been during that time that they had finally decided on what to call the car. Originally, when they had started out with the garage the idea of calling it Castle Motors, had come to them when they had been walking along Castle Road in Kidderminster not far from their workshop premises in New Road and had passed Caldwall Tower which was all that survived of an early castle built in the 14th Century. As they had walked together they had been discussing possible names for their new business. Stanley had suddenly said 'why not Castle Motors?' It had been an inspired suggestion and Laughton had agreed readily. 'Castle Motors' sounded impressive and solid! It had then seemed logical to call their car, the 'Castle Three'. He recalled that Stanley had sketched the surviving tower in pencil on the inside of a cigarette packet. The crenellated tower immediately became the new car's motif.

Meanwhile their day to day business was thriving, so fortunately, although their profits were down for 1918 they would quickly recover if they could produce the car at a sensible cost in sufficient numbers.

Castle Motors was now an official repairer approved by both the A.A. and R.A.C. and they were able to repair any make of vehicle from a 'Humble Henry' to the most luxurious. Their body shop had the capacity to build any kind of motor body whether it was for a commercial or personal vehicle. Their reputation was of being the finest equipped garage in the Midlands. Laughton felt he had rightly prided himself on being its Managing Director. This was a family business which he determined would eventually pass to provide wealth for the next generation of Goodwin.

They needed help though in planning out how the new car could be made. Stanley had brought Henry Waters, their Works Manager into their meetings which now were much more frequent,

Henry was a fresh-faced, tall thirty year old who had done his apprenticeship at Rolls Royce. He had been brought up in Kidderminster but had been forced to live in Derby whilst he had undergone his training. Throughout he had been looking around for an opportunity of work closer to where the rest of his family lived. He had approached Stanley just before the War had started and they had taken him on. His rise within the firm had been mercurial as he had displayed both engineering talents way beyond his years and also leadership. He had been Works Manager for the previous two years.

Within a short time working together the three of them had managed to produce a couple of prototypes which they had fitted with Dorman engines bought from the manufacturers.

Stanley had also managed to produce a design for an epicyclic gearbox. He was particularly proud of the design as unlike other gearboxes of that time it was both smooth to use and easily accessible for maintenance. With Henry he had spent long solitary hours in the machine shop until eventually he had solved the problems of design and tooling. Two or three prototypes had been produced. Stanley and Henry had tested them out in the car. Modest improvements were then made before Stanley had passed the gearbox as ready for full production. He had then applied for a patent to protect the intellectual property rights.

The first prototype car's bodywork Laughton recalled had been painted a cream colour which had a hint of green in it. The car was fitted with sidelights bolted onto brackets fixed to the front mudguards which were painted black. There were also headlights either side of the bonnet's brass radiator front grille which proudly bore the Castle motif on a medallion below the radiator cap. The final motif portrayed a crenellated castle tower in brown with the word 'Castle' written across the stonework in white. The windscreen, one of the many parts they had had to buy in, was fitted with a single windscreen wiper on the driver's side.

To the driver's right hand there was a wind horn mounted on the side of the bulkhead and even the passenger had a similar horn mounted on the battery housing fitted to the running board on his side. It was a handsome looking vehicle with its red leather interior and comfortable seats which could be protected from inclement weather by use of the hood.

He had reckoned they had thought of almost everything and had produced a sturdy 10 H.P. runabout that any discerning car owner would want. When they had come to look at the pricing they were pleasantly surprised and pleased to find that their costings had been shrewdly calculated and they would be able to manufacture and sell it at a significant profit. The price they had finally settled on was £250 to include the hood, screen, dynamo lighting set, horns and tools but the spare wheel and tyre would have to be priced as optional extras. They had decided payment would have to be, deposit with order, with balance on completion when the car was collected from their Kidderminster works in New Road.

When Laughton had first tried out one of the prototype cars he had found the gears silent and smooth to use without the need to double de-clutch. There were two forward gears and reverse. Amazingly, the torque produced from the engine was so great that the car would pull away from a standing start in top gear! Well certainly, when it was on the level! The Goodyear all steel wheels were interchangeable and fitted with the new pneumatic tyres being produced by Palmer Cord including the spare.

It had taken them two and a half years of experimentation before they were through but then having signed a licensing agreement with Dorman they started to produce the car in numbers. They appointed Henry Waters to be the new Production Manager and they had charged John Greensmith, their existing sales manager, with the job of selling the car. He had produced a beautiful catalogue illustrated by numerous black and white photographs showing the personnel of the Castle Motor Company Ltd and the Works, to which were later added testimonials from satisfied customers after the first few had been sold.

Sales had been slow to start with but had become brisk after the Autocar Magazine had run a very complimentary feature about the car in their August 1919 edition. After that at the Olympia Exhibition orders turned into a deluge! Even with the extensive and well equipped factory they owned they could not meet all the orders in reasonable time.

The waiting time for one of the Castle Three had by then extended to over twelve months. Many of the deposits had had to be returned after complaint about the delay although other more enthusiastic customers were prepared to wait.

Laughton recalled visiting Antwerp the following year, 1920. John had asked him and Stanley to go with him so that they could advertise the car at the Antwerp International Exhibition held to boost international trade as the City hosted the seventh modern Olympic Games. They had entered the car for one of the Exhibition's major innovative competitions. How excited they had all been when Laughton was called up by name onto the rostrum when the winners were announced to receive the prize. They had won a gold Diploma!

He recalled that it was precisely the same day as the English water polo team had won gold medals! Despite potential customers being warned about the waiting time the Exhibition produced a further one hundred orders for the car! These were placed mainly by Belgian citizens who amazingly were prepared to travel all the way to England and Kidderminster to take delivery! Financially the car and the business were doing exceptionally well. The future looked rosy.

Then disaster had struck. One Monday Victor Nott, the Company Secretary, brought to him some post that had arrived that morning.

'You had better read this Mr. Laughton.' He had simply handed Laughton a single piece of white heavy paper. It was headed 'In the High Court of Justice,

Chancery Division.' It was a writ issued by the Ford Motor Company and dated 12th August 1920.

'Sit down Vic. I need to read this carefully. Have you shown it to Stanley?'

'No not yet. I thought you should see it first. It alleges we have infringed their patent in relation to the drive mechanism on the Three.'

'Then we had better have Stanley in here. He designed the mechanism and will know the technical details probably better than me. Do we have any answer to this?'

'I have no idea Laughton. You and Stanley are the engineers not me!'

Stanley had come quickly when summoned. He too had then read the writ. Halfway through he had sat down looking distressed as the contents sunk in.

'This is dreadful!' he had finally said as he removed his reading glasses and stared with incredulity at Laughton. 'But I don't believe that I have breached their patent. I didn't even know of this patent. Surely our patent attorney should have spotted it? We are going to have to go and see him again. Maybe if we altered the line selector and brake band mechanism we could get round this. I don't know. This is all going to be very expensive. And just when the car is selling so well!'

The solicitor's letter accompanying the Writ had stated that unless they ceased the alleged infringement immediately Ford would take them to Court and seek an injunction to prevent them continuing production. It had been clear after taking immediate advice from their solicitor that they would have to give a written undertaking either to stop production or to meet any claim for damages if Ford proved their case. They had reluctantly decided that stopping production while they sorted the matter out was probably going to be the cheaper option.

Laughton recalled that a day later they had gone urgently to see their patent attorney, one of the senior attorneys of Brimfield Associates based in Birmingham. When they left Walter Andrews, the attorney in question, they had felt little wiser as to whether they had a defence or not. His advice had not seemed like advice at all! He had appeared to have just sat on the fence! Their solicitor, Robert Fox, had accompanied them. He too had been left confused by what they had been told. The conversation Stanley and he had with Robert after the meeting at Brimfield's offices was indelibly etched on Laughton's memory.

'What do you chaps want me to do?' Robert Fox had asked. 'Ford are big. They will be able to throw a lot of money you know at this. Unless you are sure we have a cast-iron defence Stanley, then you will have to think about replacing this gearbox with another one and avoiding any contentious litigation.'

Both he and Stanley had already been thinking along similar lines but had not voiced their fears. Stanley had been unusually defiant for him and said he wanted to fight as he thought the epicyclic gear box he had invented in no way had breached Ford's patent. Robert and Laughton had to talk him through the enormous costs involved in following that risky path even if they won! If they lost all that they had built would be lost. It could be a ruinous gamble. Even the personal guarantees for the capital with which they had had to finance the Castle Three might be at risk.

Eventually they had walked back with Robert to his office in Waterloo Street where after lengthy and sometimes heated discussion a decision was finally made. They would not attempt to fight but give the undertakings that Ford had asked for in the letter accompanying the writ. They would also have to pay Ford's London solicitor's costs of £850 which despite Laughton's protests, Robert said were perfectly reasonable. Stanley had agreed to find another gearbox to use in the car. They had travelled back to Kidderminster together very dejected. Fortunately Ford had not demanded that they re-call all the cars already sold! It had been their only comfort.

It had taken another eight weeks of lost production and all the costs that entailed before Stanley had found another suitable gearbox. They had eventually decided to raise new money and quite a lot of it to buy up the small firm, Wardle & Co. in Halesowen, who produced the new gearbox. They had reckoned that in the end this would be cheaper than buying the gearboxes in from them. The gearbox was already patented. Stanley had convinced Laughton that he would be able to produce improvements to the gear selection mechanism. Although as a 'crash' gearbox it would never be as smooth as Stanley's own epicyclic gearbox it would at least be robust and the best available to them at the time. In the meantime they would benefit from the profits of existing sales being made by Wardle & Co.

Production had restarted but the incident had knocked the wind out of their sails. They were even further behind with completion of orders and as the delays grew longer and longer more customers cancelled. The Castle Three somehow was not living up to its early promise in an expanding market.

Chapter 8

THE WELLS HOUSE
AND UNCLE JACK

Meanwhile back at 'The Cottage', Rachel Partridge, Mac and Barry's nanny, had done a good job within the parameters she had been set. Barry was soon to start at the nursery school down in Hagley village. The school had already begun the learning process for Mac but the time had now come to choose a preparatory school for him.

Mac had appeared to Laughton at that time to be a reasonably bright but rather diffident seven year old. Seeing him with his small group of friends from kindergarten at birthday parties and playing together it was evident that he was much liked but not as confident and hardy as Laughton himself wanted. His three R's were not full of the substance that Laughton thought his nursery school should have imbued him with by now. He went and spoke to his brother-in-law, Jack Palethorpe about which school Mac should go to.

Mac had always looked up to his Uncle Jack as a hero. Rightly so, Laughton had thought, after all as he had told Mac when he had started asking questions about the War, only brave people were given medals. Jack had been awarded the Military Cross for bravery when serving in the Royal Flying Corps in 1917 attacking singlehandedly an over-whelming force of seventeen enemy planes. His gunner was killed and Jack had landed, calmly collected a replacement gunner and taken up the attack once more! Jack's courage had enhanced his reputation in all their eyes, particularly young Mac's.

Laughton recalled Jack showing Mac the shiny bronze medal with its white ribbon and central purple stripe shortly after the King had invested him with it. Mac, then just three, had turned to him and said 'I wonder if I will ever be brave enough to win a medal like Uncle Jack, father?' He had felt a rush of the guilt at not having fought himself in the War. Muttering something about medals being only won in wartime and that he hoped Mac would never have to fight in a war he had moved the conversation on as it had become too uncomfortable for him.

Jack knew the local schools and their products. He had been in Worcestershire even longer than Laughton. When he had finally pinned Jack down to speak to, which in itself was no mean task, he was so full of news of one sort or another that it was a while before Laughton had been able to get round to the reason for his visit. Jack's answer was an immediate recommendation.

'Try and get him into The Wells House, Laughton, they will make a little man of him! You had better get on though with getting his name down. I hear they actually have a waiting list.' So he had made contact with the Head and arranged for Jessie and himself to visit the school and see for themselves what it was like.

It was a fine Spring Day. Jessie and he had driven over together in the old Hudson Super Six he had liked so much he had kept it for years. He recalled Jessie had worn a brown felt hat with a feather in it! Odd what the brain commits to memory. Arriving early for their 10 o'clock appointment, the boys were spilling over for their mid-morning break rushing about playing tag and in little groups talking intently; some of them eating what looked like bread and dripping. The bustle and obvious vibrancy of the school had been his first impression. They had gone into The Wells House itself and had been met by the Head, a chap called Philip Merryweather. Tall and strapping like Laughton himself, with warm intelligent eyes, he had come forward and shaken them both warmly by the hand before taking them into his study where papers were strewn higgledy-piggledy over every flat surface. Hanging on the air was a mixed smell of recently smoked tobacco and of ancient dust which lay on surfaces all around like a heavy grey pall. Merryweather had quickly walked to a small side table and swept up a pipe that lay there with a packet of Swan Vesta matches and thrust the pipe into his mouth.

'Excuse the muddle' he had said as he cleared a particularly big pile of papers from a large armchair whose ancient cover had a worn-bare look about it. He ushered Jessie to sit down whilst he cleared another more modest chair for Laughton.

'So you want to send young Mac here do you?' he had continued as he struck a match and re-lit his pipe putting the ball firmly into their court. The aroma of the tobacco had been very strong. Laughton's olfactory nerve recalled it even now. It had smelt like Wills Gold Flake. At this distance he could not now recall all the conversation but he had been impressed by Merryweather himself. He had set out his stall succinctly and with clarity telling them about the way in which the school operated and also efficiently dealing with the constant interruptions from the boys whose ease of access to him and affectionate respect for him was clear for all to see.

Although only in what appeared to be his mid-forties Merryweather himself actually owned the school. He told them a little of his own history which had led to him buying the school. All Laughton remembered now was that he had served as a gunnery officer and been one of just a handful of survivors when HMS

Indefatigable had been sunk under enemy fire at the Battle of Jutland. His kindly eyes constantly engaged with Laughton and Jessie. They were a startling blue and were surrounded by laughter lines. His hair was greying at the temples giving him a distinguished air as befell a Cambridge graduate.

Before the War he had taught English after University. When the War ended his father, a City banker, had died rather suddenly from a heart attack leaving him a considerable sum of money. He had decided that he would like to run his own school and had thus come to buy The Wells House which already had a formidable reputation as a school.

By the time their hour with him had come to an end Laughton was convinced that this was the right school for Mac to attend and he had told Jessie so as they returned to the car. Jessie had not been so sure. She felt that Mac's sensitivity would not find the regime which had been mapped out to them to his liking. Indeed she had gone further saying that she thought it might actually make him unhappy. He had recalled reassuring her that Mac would soon get used to the regime and that it was not unlike his own first school. A final decision was made within a few days and despite Jessie's continuing concerns, Mac's name was duly registered with the school for him to start that autumn, Michaelmas Term 1922, just a couple of months before his eighth birthday.

The memories which now leapt into Laughton's mind came from conversations with both boys mainly after they had completed their education; conversations that had occurred whilst walking or holidaying with them on Anglesey or when Mac had ridden with him. The truth had emerged not all at once but in snippets of conversation across the years and it was only now somehow that it had all come to be pieced together.

The loyalty of the child had withstood the shocks the school imposed upon him but Jessie had been right. Mac had not been particularly happy at The Wells House. He wondered for how many that had been true. He himself had acted from the best of motives and on what he had considered was the best advice at the time. What a burden parenting could be, especially in retrospect!

His first conversation with Mac and another, much later with Barry had shown how different the boys were. The first with Mac must have been when they were still living at 'Maryknowle' in Clent not long after his boy had started at The Wells House and before their move to Palmers Hill. It was a cold winter's day and they were together alone. He did not recall where the rest of the family had been. Mac was telling him about his first day at school but why he had been doing that save for the obvious reason that he was unhappy, he hadn't now any recollection. Barry had not yet started at The Wells House and Betty would still have been a toddler with her pretty blonde curls and angelic smile, her daddy's girl!

'After you left with mother I had to wait a long time before I was taken to my dormitory you know!' Mac had suddenly blurted out 'You told me it would all be great fun but all – and I mean all – the windows were open and I felt really cold. Mrs Lyons, you know the one I mean, she does the Head's typing. Well, I think she rather took pity on me for she took me into her office and we played Happy Families for a while. It was warmer there. She had a gas fire on. She told me that Matron would be along for me and that I would be in Raleigh dorm on the second floor. Turned out my dorm was between Matron's bedroom and the Head's!'

He had paused to see his father's reaction but Laughton had said nothing. Mac had plunged on 'Eventually I was taken there and found that the beds were lined up so my headboard was in the middle of the room but the boys either side had their headboards against the wall. Not like in Barry's and my room at home. My head was stuck out in the middle of the room father, and I didn't like it at all! I had to fold all my clothes just so or I was told I would be in trouble and I had to put that new red jacket you bought me on just a chair by my bed! Then next morning after breakfast I had to learn how to make my bed with something called 'hospital corners' for the sheets and blankets. Don't know why they are called that do you? S'pose something they do in hospitals! But that was after we had been woken up when the sun was still getting up and they made me throw off my warm jimjams and go just in my dressing gown to a freezing cold bathroom with the other boys and have a cold bath. Father, they pushed me down so my shoulders went in! Matron said that if I didn't do it I would get beaten! I was frozen after that; we then had our daily roll call outside in the pouring rain. Every morning it's like that! We have to reply something like 'add some' when your name is called and then we have to walk all the way uphill to Holy Well and then run back before we can have any breakfast. Then we have to sing in Chapel! And the 'uppers' and 'downers', that's what they call the lavatories, have no doors and you have to tell if you've been! Father I hate it there! Do I have to stay there? You mustn't send Barry you really mustn't' he had implored at the end of his anguished outpouring as if his entreaty for his brother would somehow imbue what he had said with added value!

Laughton had been initially rather taken aback by Mac although he had deliberately steeled himself against showing it. He recalled gently questioning Mac and finding out that the food generally was adequate and nourishing with what seemed to be a healthy emphasis on vegetables actually grown in the school's own kitchen garden. Mac had sensibly asked for more blankets for his bed and he had been given as many as he wanted. It emerged though that the school curriculum focussed on sport; football for his first term; now rugby as a prop forward and it would be cricket next term.

Mac had never been particularly interested in any sport save riding and he had never taken part in team games before. Laughton had concluded that there was nothing seriously wrong but that Mac needed to settle in. Their conversation had ended in him gently chiding Mac; telling him to buckle down and work hard and it would all be all right. Jack had said that they would make a little man of Mac and the conversation with Mac merely endorsed his view that it had all been too cosy at home with Jessie too eager to please the children.

What a difference though when he had sent Barry to join Mac a couple of years later. Barry had loved the regime at the school from day one. He had relished the sport and ignored the academic subjects they had tried to knock into him! The school was a laugh to him. Whatever they had thrown at him, be it walking, boxing, rugby or shooting Barry had entered into the activity with enthusiasm.

He had particularly liked the summer terms when the River Picnic took up a whole day. A fleet of Bedford coaches would take the whole school to Tewkesbury where an armada of small boats would be waiting for them on the Avon. Barry had been quite undaunted by the fact that his first trip on the river was at a time when he was just learning to swim and there were no life jackets! Anyway they would row themselves up to Twyning and then onto Bredon where they would moor to eat their picnic lunch; then after visiting the old Tithe Barn they would row back to their starting point for the journey back to school aboard their bus. Whilst Mac was clearly less interested in such trips than Barry even he had enjoyed that annual expedition.

But despite Laughton's best endeavours the reports that came back at the end of each term continued to give a clear indication that neither boy was particularly marked out for academic work. Comments from teachers along the lines 'tries very hard but has not made the progress we had hoped for' were legion in Mac's reports from The Wells House and for Barry it was common to read 'enjoys sport immensely to the detriment of virtually all other subjects! Must try harder next term!'

As Laughton had paid nearly £80 a term to keep the two of them at their school it had made him rather angry at times to read such comments. He had thought back to his own time at school and the lack of opportunities compared with his sons now at The Wells House. He recalled he had spoken quite harshly to both boys about the need to work hard and why they would regret it in later life when they were grown up if they didn't, but his words seemed totally to miss their targets for nothing changed save that eventually he had resigned himself to the fact that his 'boys' were not particularly interested in school work! But fortunately Mac had certainly been much happier once his younger brother had joined him. The 'boys' had always been a close support for each other.

Nevertheless, both had exhibited practical talents. Show them a car engine and start taking it apart and they were riveted to watch and could remember immediately the names of the parts and how they fitted together. In the school holidays they had loved coming down to the works with him and in a corner Jack Humphreys, his foreman mechanic, had set an old Lanchester engine on a frame together with a toolbox.

Jack Humphreys lived in Kidderminster and had worked for him from the time Castle Motors started. He had married a local girl and they had a daughter but no boys to initiate into the secret workings of automobile engines. Jack had known both the boys since they were small and was clearly very fond of them although Laughton had suspected even from that early time his favourite was Barry. It was Jack Humphries who had instructed each of the boys how to strip down the engine and put it back together.

Both Mac and Barry had taken to this unofficial engineering apprenticeship with an enthusiasm otherwise totally absent in their interest in formal education! So many times they singly or together had stripped that engine and put it back together with no apparent difficulty at all. Well it would be all right he had thought at the time. There was room in the business now for both of them although he thought Mac would be the steadier hand at the tiller when he wanted eventually to retire, so his hopes on that score had alighted on Mac to take over the firm. His hopes had never changed.

But the stripping and re-building of the Lanchester engine at the works paled into insignificance when their Uncle Jack indulged the boys by introducing them to flying. To enable him to teach them in the air Jack bought a twin seater aeroplane, an Avro 504 trainer to add to the single seater Sopwith Pup he had managed to acquire as 'surplus' after the War. This was the first time he had had a dual cockpit plane and been able to share his flying with his two nephews. Both the boys quickly became enthused with flying as were so many of their young friends. To fly was the new generation's goal and Laughton recalled how he had taken the boys to see several of the flying circus' displays when they had appeared at the nearby aerodrome which was later to become RAF Castle Bromwich.

Few boys though had an uncle who could indulge them as much as Jack used to Mac and Barry. Once home from school in the holidays they used to excitedly want to make contact with Uncle Jack and go and fly with him in his aeroplane. He had captured their imagination with his flying skills and found them a natural practical home with the constant maintenance that the Avro needed between flights. How to service the plane's engine and check it over before each flight; how to mend holes in the wings with canvas and dope! All of this they had gradually learnt from Jack who was unstinting in his praise for the two of them and allowed them far more latitude of action than Laughton would have dared to permit.

There had come a time in all this when Laughton had realised that they had both somehow picked up his engineering expertise without actually looking at a single book! But when he heard that Jack had allowed Mac to fly the plane with Jack in the back cockpit at the age of just thirteen he was seriously concerned. When he had collared Jack about it Jack was very laid back. It was just after Jack had moved to his new house, Knoll Hill, in Blakedown where he had immediately laid out a new runway on the grass at the rear in order to continue flying.

'What do you want of young Mac then Laughton?' he had started 'don't you want him to be adventurous … he can be you know? Completely at home in the air your boys, both of them. Neither of them have had a moment's air sickness! I expect Mac will be able to go solo well before he is sixteen. He can land almost faultlessly now and he is only thirteen. Look at this Laughton' he had continued 'a letter I had from him written at school. He is much happier there now Barry's there with him but I said it would be the making of him to go to The Wells House and it has!'

Jack had handed him a single sheet of writing paper written in Mac's unmistakeable hand with the fountain pen Jessie and he had given him for his last birthday. The contents, even the date 5th October 1927, were indelibly etched on his memory for he recalled it had amused and cheered him.

Dear uncle Jack

I hope you will enjoy liveing *(oh how he wished Mac could spell properly)* in your new house. *(the next bit was smudged as if Mac was going to write something and then changed his mind)* If you do sell the aeroplane will you sell it to me, *(what about a full stop my boy!)* I have saved some money in case. We are haveing *(not again!)* a jolly good term so far. We have not had any matches yet. Give my love to auntie.

With love
from
Mac

He had openly laughed despite his annoyance with the errors. The idea of Mac buying Jack's aeroplane was laughable. His savings might have bought him some tuck but not an aeroplane! But his concerns had not been allayed by Jack and they never were. Sometime when Mac had been in the RAF Reserve he had told him of his first solo flight which had taken place one Saturday when he had turned fifteen and just before they were all due to go on holiday to Rhosneiger.

He had cycled as he frequently did early in the morning across Hagley to meet Jack so he could fly with him for an hour before breakfast. The weather was still hot that week. Barry had been away at camp with the school but was due back that very day. So it had been the last opportunity for Mac to be alone with Jack for a while and not have to share his experience with his younger brother.

Jack had helped him on with his kit including a parachute and into the front cockpit where sitting on it gave him a little more height! Jack had swung the heavy single wooden propeller on Mac's signal and when Mac gave the 'thumbs up' Jack had pulled away the chocks. The Avro 504's engine quickly warmed as Jack had clambered up onto the wing and into the rear cockpit. Together they had done three circuits of the field where Jack's runway was with Jack letting Mac take the controls fully after the first. Mac had then landed dropping the plane down onto the grass runway with consummate ease. Jack had got out of the plane suddenly telling Mac with a smile that it was now time he went solo!

Mac it seemed had been taken aback with considerable apprehension when Jack had made this announcement that he was going up on his own for his first solo!

But adrenaline and excitement had quickly overcome his initial fear. Despite his apprehension he swopped over to the rear cockpit. Sitting there the aircraft would be better balanced with him flying on his own. When the engine had been restarted he had managed an almost perfect take off into the wind. His instruction had been to do a single circuit and then land but coming in for the first time he had found himself going too fast and had been forced to abort and fly round once more. Pulling back the throttle he again lined the Avro up to land and brought her down with a bounce and then a three point landing eventually taxiing to a halt near where Jack had been watching.

'Not bad for a first go,' Jack had declared. 'Better not tell your father or he will think I am being reckless again with you!' Mac had been brimming over with exhilaration. He had instantly recalled his father's earlier anxiety and that is why his first youthful flight had remained a secret for many years. Of course, he had told Barry and sworn him to secrecy. Barry then only thirteen had been easily persuaded to keep the secret because he too hoped that Jack would let him fly on his own when he reached Mac's age! Mac indeed had recalled how the following Saturday when both boys had gone to meet Uncle Jack, Barry had pestered for an immediate solo flight but had been told he would have to wait until he was older and had been distinctly disappointed!

Chapter 9

CASTLE FOUR AND DISASTER

Production of the Castle Three was still well behind schedule and more customers had become fed up with waiting and had demanded the return of their deposits. What with repaying the loans he and Stanley had taken out to buy Wardle and Co. and the overall costs of lost production they were coming under increasing financial pressure. The modifications to the Wardle gearbox had taken far longer than either he or Stanley had ever envisaged. Also the size and weight of the new gearbox had necessitated re-design of the chassis mountings. This meant that they had been forced to alter the existing chasses already laid down. The modifications had taken yet further costly time out of production.

He recalled too how Stanley had never been really happy once the Castle Three had been modified. He frequently complained that his original design had been compromised by the modifications that had been forced upon them. The gearbox was not the epicyclic gearbox that had been his 'baby' and the feel of the car was inferior to that of the original.

Meanwhile the Austin motor company had produced a sturdy little four seater called the 'Seven'. Stanley had already anticipated such a market development by producing a design for a Castle Four. Laughton acknowledged that it was an inspired design but the costings had not been favourable and he thought they should go back to their core business of servicing and repairing motor vehicles and cut their losses.

Stanley though had disagreed and wanted to produce the Castle Four to replace the Castle Three despite the huge capital costs involved to produce his new car. The brothers had clashed about the way forward several times neither being prepared to give way.

Laughton had not wanted to fall out with Stanley. He thus decided to gain some time by allowing Stanley to build two prototypes of the Four. With good fortune by the time that was done Laughton would be better able to gauge how the market was developing. Both of them could then make the right decision and they could do it together. But he recalled as both at that time had an equal shareholding in Castle Motors, the business for a time had reached an impasse!

Then something had happened that was to change everything. It was past midnight when the knock came at the door. He would have slept on but Jessie hearing it jolted him awake.

'Laughton it's someone at the door.'

Awake he glimpsed at the wind-up alarm clock at the side of their double bed. It was 1.25am. He recalled how he had then rushed downstairs and by the moonlight had seen the bluish tinge of a Police helmet through the frosted glass in the small pane of the front door. A sense of foreboding had come over him.

'Mr Goodwin?' the uniformed officer had asked as he opened the front door.

'Yes,' he had replied 'What on earth are you doing waking me at this hour?' Fear had coloured his normal equilibrium with a wholly unreasonable anger.

'I am sorry sir; it's your factory in New Road. There's a fire and we need you down there. Your foreman, Jack Hilton, your key holder, he's already down there helping the fire brigade but I am afraid that they do not have the blaze under control as yet.'

The quiet modulation of the officer's voice announcing this catastrophe somehow had altered his mood and his usual calmer self had taken command again.

'Give me a minute officer. I'll throw on some clothes and come with you. Come along in and sit yourself down I won't be a moment.'

Returning upstairs he found that Jessie had overheard the conversation. Practical as ever she was in her dressing gown and whilst he quickly dressed she went down and by the time he had returned downstairs she was in the kitchen making some hot coffee and a few cheese sandwiches for him to take with him. Funny that he should remember precisely all these years later that they were cheese sandwiches! The boys had not woken and quickly saying 'goodbye' to Jessie, not knowing when he would be back he was on his way with the officer. Odd thinking back he never did know that officer's name even though he was obviously from the Hagley Police Station. He thought he had known them all.

Several streets before they had arrived in New Road he had smelt the acrid fumes of the fire. They had parked a hundred yards or so away in Pump Street and then walked to turn into New Road itself. As they walked out of the protective cool of the buildings on the corner the factory opposite him came into view. But it was the intense heat of the blazing inferno that he felt first and he had to protect his head and eyes from the particles of fire blown dust that with the bluster of the breeze were everywhere. The noise was almost deafening; the crackling of roof joists and timbers as the fire flamed high into the sky; the odd crump of a small explosion of an oxygen cylinder used by the welders; all that coupled with the whoosh of the fireman's nozzles and pumps as thousands of gallons of water were plied to the task of extinguishing the fire.

Inspector Joseph was with Jack Hilton in the lee of the heat. They recognised him immediately and had come to him. The Inspector acknowledged his subordinate who then left the three of them standing there.

'Bad business this Mr Goodwin,' the Inspector had said loudly above the noise of the fire, 'best keep well back until the firemen have things under control' and he ushered them well back away from the immediacy of the fire.

'What started it?' Laughton had asked also shouting to make himself heard as he surveyed the ruins of No 1 Machine Shop.

'We won't know until it's all out but they think that it started over there.' The Inspector had replied and had pointed.

'In the Paint and Finishing Shop,' he had come back, 'yes that makes sense; there are lots of inflammable materials in there!'

The Inspector had left him then. The hopelessness of it all struck him. All Stanley's paper design work all gone up in flames and the factory rendered useless for, well how long would it take to come back from this disaster; a very long time. Then a thought had come to him. Stanley's prototype Castle Four would have been in the store next to the Paint Shop. He himself had never wanted to produce a four wheeler. It looked now as if he would get his way.

The direct and indirect costs of dealing with the Ford patent action, the costs and engineering difficulties of producing the replacement gearbox had taken their toll. All that and now this disastrous fire which would take further months out of their production schedule. It looked as if their car production had now come to an abrupt end. He recalled smiling grimly as the repercussions of the thought sank in.

Jack Hilton still by him, filled him in as to what had been happening before he arrived. It turned out that his foreman had arrived just as the fire was beginning to take hold in the paint shop. He had realised that he needed to act fast if anything was to be saved. Despite being told not to go into the burning premises he had managed to get into the store next to the main area of the fire through the back doors. It was with some pride that he had told Laughton that he had managed to save both prototype Castle Fours and that they were sitting parked up the road. The one without an engine he had pushed outside by himself but then he had managed to persuade a bystander to help him push it from the yard at the back of the factory onto the road and well away from the fire.

As they had talked a lady from the houses nearby whom he had recognised by her wispy blonde hair and a likeness he could not place came over to them. She was carrying a tray with steaming hot mugs of tea on it. Her gait was such that some of the tea would never reach them but he was taken by her kindness.

'Thought you might be better for this,' she had said as she had nodded at the tea. 'Sorry about all that,' she added with another nod towards the factory still burning and crackling behind them.

'You must be Mr Laughton?' she had said to him. 'You're the one who gave my young Bert a chance of work before he went off to the War.'

He had then remembered the likeness. Of course, Bert Goodrich, who had come to him as an engineering apprentice had borne that same nose and smile. He had only been sixteen when War had broken out. One day he had not turned up for work and Laughton recalled a distraught father coming to his office looking for him. It turned out that he had run away to join up. Later he had heard that apart from a postcard to say that he was in France somewhere that was the last his parents had heard of him until they had received a telegram saying that he had been killed in the Battle of Arras. He had written to them when he had seen Bert's name in the Kidderminster Shuttle amongst the list of those killed.

'Yes, I am Laughton Goodwin, Mrs Goodrich. Thank you, the tea is very kind of you, most welcome.' he had said as he and Jack each helped themselves to one of the steaming mugs and stirred in a spoonful of sugar. Laughton was reminded of the sandwiches still in his coat pocket. He was going to be here for some time. They would keep.

She was smiling at his recognition of her. 'Bert always said how kind you were to him Mr Laughton. It's nothing!'

'I remember your son Mrs Goodrich. He was an able craftsman and would have made a sound engineer had he lived. We were all very sad when he was killed.'

'He were a hero you know Mr Laughton.' 'They were all heroes' he had replied.

'No I mean a real hero Mr Laughton. He were awarded a medal post .... posthum...' she had stopped.

'Posthumously?' he had filled in for her.

'Yea that's the word. I knew it were a long one Mr Laughton. 'It were a Military Medal for him being brave.'

'A Military Medal?' he rejoined wondering what young Bert had done to merit such a prestigious award which he thought was only awarded to officers and inviting a reply.

'Yea. He were with his platoon following a tank. There were this machine gun firing at them. He was losing his mates. 'spect he got angry! He ran and jumped on them Germans what were doing the firing. Killed the lot of 'em. Did him no good though 'cause he got shot too.' And Laughton remembered her eyes welling with tears and her excusing herself and going back to her house. He had been left then wondering how he would feel if he lost one of his own sons.

As a pink dawn had come up the scale of the disaster had hit him. He recalled how by then Jack's place at his side had been taken by Stanley when he had arrived soon after daybreak. As they had talked he had been surprised to find that Stanley was not in the least put out about the loss of his new designs.

'Oh those,' he had said when Laughton had broken the news of the loss to him, 'they were only the final drawings. I have a full set of the preliminary ones at home. I can soon put together another set. But why are you fretting about those? You never wanted us to build it anyway!'

There had been other conversation that he no longer recalled which had led up to an uneasy silence between them. Then as if spotting a truth he had not recognised before Stanley had said, 'That's it isn't it Laughton? You didn't want the Castle Four when I started it and you don't want it now. This,' he had spread his arm in a gesture to take in the flames that still licked at the roof in front of them 'this is just the ticket for you. We shall never be able to produce any more Threes let alone a Four?'

Laughton was stung by the accuracy of Stanley's insight. He had tried to reassure him that they would come back from this as they had from the other blows but it was a half-hearted attempt and they both knew it. They ended up having an almighty row which ended when Stanley had said 'I have had enough of your machinations. You sort this out with the insurers and just give me my share of the money. I will start a garage or do something useful on my own from now on.'

With that he had stumbled away clearly upset and Laughton realised he had lost not only the factory but now also his brother. They had been inseparable as boys learning the ways of life; as young men embarking on Castle Motors and then the Castle Three. He recalled how on many later family occasions he had tried to put matters right between them but the years had passed and although they had contact with each other they never regained the closeness of those early days when together they had been such a successful partnership.

Chapter 10

LAUGHTON GOODWIN & CO.

Laughton had immediately realised he needed to talk to Victor Nott and tell him that Castle Motors was at an end. He and Stanley surely would remain still reasonably wealthy men for the insurance policy would at least cover the buildings and equipment whilst they decided what they would each do next. Victor told him that as Castle Motors was a limited company and thus a separate legal entity, they would need a company meeting to sort out the split of assets between him and Stanley. He had also mooted the idea that they might be able to sell Castle Motors.

In the event a number of Board Meetings were necessary, some of which had been rather acrimonious. Meanwhile the insurers and their assessors had been making a meal of sorting out the costs involved in re-building the factory which had been almost completely destroyed in the fire. It had even been necessary to demolish some of the walls left standing as they were deemed unsafe. There were arguments as well about the value of the machines and other equipment much of which was comparatively new.

Eventually though, it had all been sorted. It had taken over a year. The New Road factory premises had been rebuilt. After some haggling with various potential buyers, the premises had been sold to a firm of carpet manufacturers. Laughton felt that he and Stanley had been additionally fortunate in also managing to sell the Castle Motor Company and its goodwill to three former employees who had wanted to strike out on their own Bert Bagshaw, Bill Underwood and Jack Bristow.

They had taken over the premises in Vicar Street, Kidderminster and The Tything in Worcester as part of the deal. Of course, they were not manufacturers but had made a healthy business at least for a while servicing the Castle Threes which had been sold locally. They also sold motor cycles which later became their prime business. Taking in other partners at that time they had changed their trading name to BBU & Co and Castle Motors had ceased to exist.

Both he and Stanley had used their share of the monies once the Bank had been paid, to set themselves up as independent automobile engineers. He had leased premises in George Street and re-employed many of the mechanics who

41

had worked for them at New Road. He had found a new happiness in being back with what he knew in its entirety, maintaining and repairing motor cars. He had decided he was never going to be involved again in all the legal hassle of being a limited company but would simply trade under his own name. Whilst managing to retain the title of approved AA and RAC repairers he had continued his love affair with American cars.

After some negotiation he had managed to obtain the Midland Distributorship for Chrysler cars. To that he had later added District Agencies for Austin, Rover and Hillman. Stanley meantime had set himself up as a limited company under his own name with premises in Worcester Road and was selling and repairing Vauxhall and Bedford motor vehicles as a main dealer. The motor trade was really taking off and business for both of them had been brisk.

Within months Laughton had been making a profit again. As the months went by his profits increased beyond his wildest dreams. He actually started to be glad about the fire which had brought his role as a manufacturer to a premature end. This was the business he was at home with and enjoyed.

The austerity imposed on him and Jessie for the time during which they were recovering from the effects of the fire and having to part from Stanley had been hard. Jessie had been careful. Torn clothes and worn socks had been mended with care rather than replaced. Shepherd pies made out of the minced leftovers of Sunday joints and baked apples from the orchard had become regular parts of their diet. She had always been there at night awake at his side to offer him comfort by talking to him or by making love with him when he was unable to sleep. Issues about the insurance pay-out or whether they should sell Castle Motors and whether in the event they would ever be able to sell it had so preyed on his mind then. Jessie had brought him safely through even the crisis of confidence he had felt in his ability. But now all that could be seen as a temporary setback. Once again he was back on top. The family lifestyle could benefit from the rich rewards of his growing business. Now he could make it up to her and the family.

The first year's trading went so well at the garage that they were able to afford a holiday on the continent. They chose Paris. It was a hot two weeks that they spent there traipsing round the sights. The hotel they had stayed at was in Montmartre near the Sacre Coeur, its magnificent white marbled dome visible from the balcony of their room. Minding the children who were in a separate room adjoining theirs had meant they had stayed in during the evenings but they had not minded as their days were so exciting.

They had visited all the major sights including the Arc de Triumphe at the western end of the broad Champs-Elysees. He had bought Jessie some Chanel perfume from one of the exclusive shops that bordered that elegant tree-lined thoroughfare. The boys' favourite had been the Eiffel Tower and their ride up the three hundred odd feet to the top platform from which they had been able to look out over the City. From there they had walked to the Dome des Invalides nearby and seen Napoleon's tomb and then along the Seine to eat lunch at an outside table in the sun watching the traffic pass. And that was just one day! It was on that first trip abroad that Mac had fallen in love with hot croissants and that ghastly French habit of dipping them in his bowl of coffee for breakfast! They were very full days and that holiday had properly marked the restoration of the Goodwin fortunes.

There had been many, many more holidays in the summers that followed and in the winters, skiing at Grindelwald. Some of the holidays had been much more expensive but none had eclipsed the memories he had of that first one in Paris.

Still living at "The Cottage" they had realised that they needed a house where the boys would have greater freedom and could enjoy growing up in more spacious surroundings. Staff could be accommodated more easily without them being intrusive. He and Jessie could now afford a real gentleman's residence with its accompanying lifestyle. They had discussed the locality where they wanted to live.

Both had agreed that they wanted to stay in Hagley which they now knew so well. It was away from Kidderminster town with its noise and bustle; away too from meeting people who Laughton would see in business. It had kept its identity as a tiny village with just a few shops and a pub or two; yet there was the rail station which Laughton had used for some time, with trains which could get him easily to Birmingham or even London. Hagley was also surrounded by lovely Worcestershire open farming country where riding and hunting were favourite pursuits.

Laughton had always ridden since he was young but over the last few years for one reason or another he had not been able to ride with any regularity. Now he had hoped that he could make the time and realise his long-term dream of hunting with the Albrighton Woodland Hunt. Jessie had once told him that she had always fancied the idea of him in a red hunting jacket! But first they needed a house!

Chapter 11

PALMERS HILL

From time to time Jessie and he had walked at the weekends. They would walk several miles around the fields and paths of Hagley and on the Clent hills. Sometimes the boys would come with them. The boys especially loved it when he found trees for them to climb. On one occasion when they had taken a picnic they had been particularly excited when he had helped them build a den in some woodland.

He recalled that his first visit to the further reaches of Brake Lane had been on such an occasion when the family was out. It must have been in the summer of 1924 when Betty was just a toddler and both her brothers were pupils at the Wells House in Malvern.

He had never gone beyond the station in Brake Lane before. This Hagley station was where he frequently caught the train into Birmingham. Now they walked further along. There were only a few houses up there and on the left side towards the top end of the lane he saw that there was a rising piece of land on the left which would be the perfect place to build a house. He thought at the time that it must be several acres. He had wondered if it belonged to the Cobhams. He thought that the farm opposite was definitely part of their estate as it was painted in the same mid-blue as all the estate buildings near 'The Cottage'.

As the children played in the newly harvested corn field at the end of the lane, he had lain on the rug they had brought with them lapping up the still warm sun and contemplated the idea of buying that plot. Jessie and the boys obviously liked it here. It was quiet and peaceful set away from the village and whilst the plot was wooded it was surrounded by open farmland. Good for shooting and hunting he thought. He decided to say nothing to Jessie but to make a few enquiries first.

The next day he telephoned the estate office and spoke to Lord Cobham's agent there, Bill Lovelace. Bill was a man of many parts who had survived the War although he had taken a bad shrapnel wound to his left leg at Paschendale in 1917. He now walked with a permanent limp. He lived with his wife near "The Cottage" on the estate itself with their two sons. Laughton knew him through occasionally going to have a pint in the Lyttelton Arms which they shared as their local. Bill had put him in touch with various tradesmen who worked for the estate who he had employed to repair timbers and decorate some of the rooms at "The Cottage" when they had refurbished it to match their own taste.

The telephone had rang for some time before it was answered by Bill himself. 'Hello Bill, this is Laughton Goodwin here. Haven't spoken to you for a while. How are you?'

'Well enough Laughton but with the rain these last few days the leg has been giving me gyp! And what can I do for you on this Monday morning?'

Typical of his class thought Laughton not to reciprocate the pleasantries. But he suppressed the thought. He needed Bill's help.

'Jessie and I were walking in Brake Lane yesterday.'

'Oh yes its nice up there at this time of the year.'

'There is some woodland rising on the left. Bit of a hill,' he had continued. 'I wondered if the estate owned it.'

'Are you talking about Palmers Hill?'

'I have no idea.' He had answered not having heard the name before.

'Up on the left towards the top of the lane where it peters out in the field we cut last week?'

'Yes that's right. Does the estate own that?' Laughton repeated.

'Yes it does. Funny you should be ringing me at this time though because my governor was saying to me just last week that he was looking to sell part of that woodland. Seems he wants shot of it as it produces no real income. I haven't yet got round to instructing the agents to sell it. Why? Do you want to buy it?'

Laughton was a bit taken aback by Bill's incisive perception. He pressed on.

'Well I would like to take a closer look at it but perhaps yes, perhaps.'

'Why don't you go and have a good look at it then and come back to me if you're interested. There's no particular urgency as far as the estate is concerned but let me know in a couple of weeks one way or the other.'

'Right I will do that. Perhaps meet you in the Arms and buy you a pint.'

'Look forward to it Laughton.'

The conversation had ended thus. So the estate did own it and might sell it.

The next call he had made was to Richard Crumpton who he knew through riding and the purchase of the premises in New Road. Richard was not there so he had spoken to his partner Neill Young. Neill had a reputation of being a shrewd estate agent and auctioneer so Laughton was happy to ask him about the value of land in Hagley. He outlined what he wanted to know. Neill was cautious as he did not know that particular area but had said that arable land in Hagley was selling at auction for about £300 or a little more an acre and woodland for a building plot he thought might go for a little more. Laughton decided that he would discuss this idea now with Jessie and then bide his time and wait awhile before broaching the subject again with Bill. He had better make sure that he was in the Arms next Friday night to buy him a pint but he would not get drawn into conversation about the land. If he did he was sure he would have to pay more for it!

That night after the children had been put to bed upstairs and before they ate he had laid out his plan to Jessie; that they should buy enough land in Brake Lane for a large house and then get some good local architects to design them a home that was worthy of the site. Jessie's positive reaction pleased him.

'Oh Laughton, how exciting; that is a brilliant idea. We could decide exactly what rooms we needed and plan our own home exactly as we want it. I would want a modern kitchen with an electric oven and a copper. You could have a Gun Room to store your collection of guns. Can we afford it?' she asked and then as an afterthought she added. 'Perhaps we could draw on some of my trust monies. I could buy the plot and you would then have your money to build the house.'

'I am not sure that's a good idea; remember that money is really for a rainy day. We should be able to manage provided that the estimates are not too high. We have recovered from the fire losses and sales are up this year. I am doing all right now. Provided we keep a tight control on the spending as they build we should be fine. Of course, we may have to sell this first and move to rented accommodation for a while. And we may have to borrow some money on mortgage but then doesn't everyone these days in our position? But the first thing is for us to go next Sunday afternoon to Brake Lane and look at the land to see if it would be suitable for a house. If we both think it is then I will try and buy it.'

'It may be difficult for me on Sunday afternoon. The boys are going to a party but how about Saturday after you finish work? It will still be light and we could take the children with us.'

Bill was rather fortuitously not at the Arms that particular Friday. On the Saturday he had excused himself from work earlier than normal. They had put the children in the big Hudson Phantom he was driving by then. He had then driven them all down to Brake Lane. He had parked by the wooden rickety five bar farm gate which clearly led into the woodland area up the hill. There was no padlock so they opened it and entered.

'What did you say Bill called it dear?' asked Jessie as she handed Betty to him before they walked up the incline.

'No come on you can walk a bit Betty.' he had said putting Betty down. 'He said it was called Palmers Hill.'

'What a pretty name. If we live here that is what we should call it Laughton, 'Palmers Hill'.'

The boys overhearing their conversation picked up the name and Mac started to chant it as he ran up into the wood; Barry chasing after him was having difficulty with his 'p's' at that time; he could only manage 'almers' Hill! Jessie and he had laughed as the boys disappeared from view amongst the autumnal browns shushing the fallen leaves with their young feet as they ran.

The plot was plenty big enough. His initial estimate of four acres had later turned out not so far from being correct. He saw that there was ample room for quite a large house, perhaps a tennis court and a swimming pool, although those probably would have to wait until funds became available. There would be room away from the house for stabling for his hunter and perhaps one or two horses if the boys showed interest when they were a bit older.

Within the deeper part of the wood he could construct a range where he could shoot and teach the boys the rudiments of the sport when they were older. All in all it was just what he had been looking for. Jessie could not see the house in her mind's eye as well as he could, but she had liked the site and the potential hours of fun and freedom that would provide for the children as they grew up. They had agreed they should try and buy it.

He had kept to his strategy and not contacted Bill straightaway. He had decided to wait until the end of the following week. Then on the Wednesday he had been surprised to get a call from Bill himself.

'Hello Laughton. Been to see the land yet up at Palmers Hill?'

'Yes Bill I went last Saturday with Jessie and the children.'

'And?'

'We liked it and if it comes up for sale then we would like to buy it.'

'That's why I'm ringing. The governor came in yesterday after his holiday. I had a word with him about it. He would be happy to sell it to you privately and cut out the agent's fees if you make him a sensible offer. You will be wanting to put a house on it, won't you?'

Laughton carefully ignored that last question and went to the nub.

'What would he regard as a 'sensible offer' Bill?'

'I can't say Laughton, that's up to you.'

'Oh come on Bill, he recently sold some of the land over near the Hall. You must know how much it's worth.'

'That land was different it was arable land. You can't build a house there! And its more than my job's worth to divulge that sort of information, you must know that.'

Laughton was annoyed and impressed all at the same time. Annoyed with himself for he was being outmanoeuvred by Bill when he had hoped to get a cheap price immediately settled that Cobham would accept; impressed with Bill who was showing why Cobham had made such a wise choice in putting him on! He had felt forced into saying.

'All right then give me a few days and I will come back to you with an offer.'
'Right Laughton I'll wait to hear from you.'

Undeterred, he had eventually managed to talk to Chris who had been good enough to come out and meet him at Palmers Hill. Over a drink afterwards back at 'The Cottage' he had given Laughton a bracket figure value for the plot. He had also measured it within the fence lines that existed at 3 acres and 19 perches. Laughton had taken a bit off the figure and had made his offer which had been refused. Eventually after a bit of to-in and fro-in a figure of £1,150 had been agreed. This was a much higher figure than he had anticipated and he had worried whether they were taking on too much.

Partly because of that, Jessie had eventually persuaded him to let her contact Herbert Smith, one of the trustees, who managed her trust monies. The trustees had agreed to release to Jessie enough money for her to buy the land. He recalled that that was what she had wanted all along and she was overjoyed that some of her money was being invested in their new home. The family solicitors, Huggins and Co. in Birmingham sorted out the legal formalities with Cobham's solicitors who he recalled were in London. It had taken an age as the title he was told was complex.

But eventually, after signing numerous documents, he and Jessie had been told everything had been completed. He had received the lawyer's bill with incredulity. It had cost him nearly a quarter of what the land was worth to get it transferred! There was no point in arguing. They were lawyers and you did not argue or it cost you more! Hadn't he found that out in their dealings with Ford's solicitors?! He had paid the bill for Palmers Hill but been like a bear with a sore head for a few days about it.

Chapter 12

THE BUILDING OF PALMERS HILL

They had decided to sell 'The Cottage' and move to rented accommodation so releasing their capital to build. Perhaps on reflection they had moved too early but they had not anticipated how quickly 'The Cottage' would sell. In any event they had outgrown it and needed a bigger property. They had spotted a house on the Clent hills, called 'Maryknowle' which had four bedrooms and a garden big enough for the children to play in. Its lease was just up and they had been able to move there by early in the May.

He had meanwhile contacted a Birmingham firm of architects who had been recommended to him; he forgot by whom now, it was so long ago. He and Jessie had spent many hours with bits of paper putting their own ideas together for the design of the house. They had met the architect, Joseph Brayne, more times than he could remember; so many that they had soon been on Christian name terms. He had been struck by the patience of the chap as Jessie changed her mind so many times about all sorts of details, even the position of the rooms! Her charm had always carried off the proposed changes but towards the end he had thought even Joe's patience was showing slight signs of raggedness. At last they were there and the final plans were in their hands. There it was on paper; a six bedroom, two bathroom gentleman's residence with every feature that they had ever dreamed of in one house, Palmers Hill.

Finding a builder to build it was more difficult than he could possibly have imagined. He had wanted someone who really cared about what they built, to build their home. But scour the local area and widely seek contacts as he did, he could not for the life of him find a firm who had the manpower and expertise required. The architects had almost as much difficulty as he did. Many firms would not quote. Others had so much work that they were simply not interested. Still others came and quoted but their quotes were not acceptable. But eventually the architects found a firm with the right mix.

It was a Worcester family firm, Groom and Son who had been building houses since 1850. After one or two site meetings with the proprietor, Humphrey Groom, an acceptable quotation was submitted to him.

He had liked Humphrey as a down to earth kind of man who had similar thoughts to his own when it came to considering the detail of the architect's drawings; who always turned up when he said he would and who was smart in his appearance. His grandfather had started the firm and it had been passed down to Humphrey by family circumstances. He had had little formal education himself but had served a five year apprenticeship with a firm in Winchester where he had learnt all his many skills working in wood and stone. He had told Laughton proudly on one occasion how he had worked on stone mullion repairs at the cathedral there.

Humphrey had only returned to Worcester when his father started to ail with some sort of tumour and had died prematurely. The firm was now run by himself and two brothers who had survived the War, his eldest brother, Arnold having been killed at Passchendaele. For Laughton who now was an officer in the Army Reserve that was an important detail and it had clinched his choice. He thought Humphrey was somehow heaven sent.

But it was not until late 1924 that building actually could start. Apparently the bricks which were made in Dudley were a speciality hand cast red brick which it was difficult to get in the numbers that were required. Humphrey had put his senior foreman, Alan Jones in charge of the job.

Alan was a handsome chap in his mid thirties. He had recently married a local girl called Shirley. They had one young daughter about Betty's age and another on the way. Once the job had started there had never been anything Alan had not been able to do or organise; no difficulty that he could not deal with or get round. Full of personal initiative and common sense his catchphrase seemed always to be 'press on regardless'; the sort of approach which had resonated with Laughton who admired those like himself who had that drive.

It had taken a while to set up the site even before any actual building work started. Grooms first task was to construct the planned drive up to the existing glade which was at the top of the rise. It was on this more level area that Palmers Hill would eventually stand. Tons of stone were brought from a nearby quarry to form the bed of the drive which had to be strong enough to take both horse and motor traffic. They had used a small mechanical digger to excavate the passage for the drive.

Although there were still some men working as well as the digger the method was nothing like the way in which he had seen roads being built before such motorised diggers had been available. Then hordes of men had done the work but sadly he mused the War had put paid to all that! Without the digger now he was not sure how matters would have gone.

They worked solidly on the driveway which had neared completion after a couple of weeks. Then Alan Jones established a sort of base camp at the top of the drive. Some wooden sheds were erected. One was to become Alan's office.

Another was to house tools. He recalled three. The last must have been for the men to meet at meal times. Other areas became storage areas filled with deliveries of sand and gravel. An earth privy was positioned a little way away at the edge of where some elm and oak trees had been felled to enlarge the site.

An open wooden structure was erected near the foreman's shed to store all the wood supplies needed for the house. There were huge solid roof timbers and floor joists; floor boards, skirting boards and architraves. It was a shame that they could not use some of the oak that had been felled. They had managed to sell that timber to keep the prices down but it was still a sizeable bill for all the timber which would be required. He had paid it in one of the early stage payments which had been presented to him. When he had queried as to whether it was all needed at that time Alan had explained that it was; to enable the wood to continue seasoning so that by the time the joiners and carpenters came to use it there would be less risk of it warping.

He visited most days to see what was happening. Sometimes he took one or both of the boys in the Hudson. Betty usually was left at home with Jessie. The boys would go off and play in the woodland or chat to the workmen while he talked to Alan. One day he recalled he had been up there and a couple of labourers were digging out some sort of shallow pit near the site which was now levelled off ready to have the lines of the building marked out. The brown flattened earth looked rather as he had seen the piece of tweed laid out flat on the cutting table pricked out with chalk at his tailors prior to it being cut out to make the sports jacket he was now wearing.

The boys had leapt from the car as soon as he had parked and having spotted the workmen digging they had rushed over to find out whether this was going to be the swimming pool. He had already told them several times that the swimming pool would have to wait along with his ideas for a tennis court and a shooting range but they had been much too excited to recall any earlier conversation on the topic!

Tom the lead labourer was always very patient with them. He knew boys. After all he and his Bessie had four and two girls as well! As he wandered over in ignorance to hear for himself why the pit was required, he had heard Tom teasing the boys telling them it was to house all the elves from the wood who needed new homes now that Palmers Hill was being built! He had smiled at the use of the name. All the workmen had picked up the name Jessie had first thought of for their new home and he had even overheard in the local pub a couple of them refer to it as such over a pint.

Eventually he had persuaded Tom to tell the boys the real purpose for the pit being dug. No good any of them not understanding these things. Part of the boys and his own education was how he had regarded it. After all, this would be their family home and eventually he hoped Mac's, long after he had gone. So the boys had to stand by him Barry idling his foot in the soil he stood on while the explanation was given. Mac more serious and that bit older had held his hand and listened intently.

It turned out that the pit was going to be a lime pit. It was needed as a source of slaked lime which they would use to make the plaster for the internal walls and mortar to put between the bricks which still had not arrived. Limestone already burnt in a lime kiln would be brought up the drive when delivered and dumped into the pit. Then it would be immersed in water and left to marinate for a few weeks. This 'putty lime' as it was apparently called would then be ready to use in the mortar.

The boys ran off to play and Alan had called him over to make sure they stayed away from the pit and the well that had been finished the week before and was about to be lined with bricks. Alan had brought in a chap who specialised in such linings as Grooms did not employ anyone who could do it. The well would supply the water needed for the building work and later the house itself. Electricity lines were already in Brake Lane so by negotiation with the supplier Alan had managed to get power brought onto the site. It would give light in the sheds and power the pump yet to be installed at the side of the well.

By the beginning of March the preparation was complete. Building Palmers Hill then started in earnest. Grooms were traditional builders but had tried to move with the times. They had recently acquired one of the latest Model T Ford lorries. It was proudly possessed and kept immaculate despite the heavy everyday wear and tear to which it was subjected. Painted in dark brown each door announced their name in white letters. Occasionally, when he and the boys had been there, Tom would tell Mac and Barry that the lorry was expected. They would run down the metalled driveway and wait expectantly at the gate leading onto the road.

Sometimes they had to wait for quite a long time, but then the note of a labouring engine would be heard, as the burdened lorry trundled slowly up the unmade lane and swung into the driveway entrance. Bill Bates was the usual driver. The boys would be perched on the gate and ride it as he opened it. Then they would clamber up into the passenger seat. Before letting off the handbrake Bill would crunch the gear into first and they would make the steady climb up the knoll. Their faces always had seemed to reflect the fun they felt in being involved!

The site was now pegged out and the labourers led by Tom dug out the foundations. The spoil was barrowed up a plank onto the lorry and taken off the site. Laughton recalled that is how he first came to have contact with Felix Wilkes who later had become such a close friend. The Wilkes family farmed the arable land the other side of Brake Lane opposite Palmers Hill and when Felix, saw that there was stony subsoil to be had he had come across and approached Alan asking for it to be dumped to make up the potholes along the track leading to the farm. Alan of course had asked Laughton and he had gone over and met Felix.

First impressions had been of a rather gruff farmer who just managed to produce enough income from the land to keep himself and his family financially buoyant. But then Laughton had not known many farmers at that time. When he did he had found out they were all a bit like that! Only later did he realise that Felix and his wife, Helen, were salt of the earth characters upon whom you could rely in the darkest times. They were to become frequent visitors to Palmers Hill. His first encounter with Felix about the waste had suited them both; not too far to have to take the spoil; free subsoil for Felix and longer and more frequent trips in the lorry when the boys were there!

The foundations went down about three feet in most places before the architect and the local authority building surveyor concurred that they had found a suitable load-bearing layer deep enough not to shrink. Although bricks were still being used for foundations and were favoured by the builder, the architect had advised him finally to use concrete. A small petrol powered mixer had arrived on site soon afterwards. The plonk–plonk of its four stroke engine sounded all day as it mixed the large quantities of concrete necessary to fill the two foot six inch wide strip foundations to the architect's requested depth of nine inches. In some places where extra strength was required it was even deeper. They allowed a couple of weeks for it all to harden and then the bricklayers had arrived.

Each labourer served two bricklayers bringing them bricks on hods as the cavity walls took shape; red facing bricks for the outside leaf and less expensive commons for the inside. Now all day and every day the site was full of activity. Gradually as the rows of bricks mounted, the house started to rise from the ground. Outside the main structure underground drains had been built using interlocking salt glazed stoneware pipes which led to a cess pit. It would all be joined up eventually to the various internal drains. As spring gave way to summer, fresh cold sparkling mornings gave way to longer sun filled days. It was a hot summer that year. The labourers removed their shirts and worked as their bodies sweated and tanned in the heat. There would be friendly banter between them as they worked. The banter would stop abruptly when he went over to see how things were progressing. He noticed that they seemed more willing to talk to the boys than him!

Then one Saturday he and Jessie had gone over at Alan's behest. He said he had a surprise for them. The boys and Betty had come too. He recalled how all of them had been excited. Alan did not usually ask them to go over on Saturdays although they often did go and look over the site at weekends as Jessie liked to see how far things had moved on. They usually picked Sundays to visit as then the site was quiet. Most Saturdays the men worked. This Saturday they arrived as bidden at eleven in the morning to find that Humphrey Groom and Alan were there waiting for them. After the usual pleasantries Humphrey had led them all over to where the base of the house had emerged above the damp proof course and where the loggia eventually would stand. There on the ground had been a small sandstone block. Chiselled into it were his and Jessie's initials and the year; L.C.G and J.G. and underneath 1925. A foundation stone. They had had to explain what that was to the boys. For as long as Palmers Hill stood and whoever lived there, all would know that it was built in 1925 by their father and mother. Alan had produced a bucket of mortar and a trowel. Jessie had given the trowel to Mac first and then to Barry.

'Go on put some cement in there' she said pointing to the gap in the brickwork where the stone was to be placed. Each of the boys in turn, a bit half heartedly, had slopped some mortar onto the bricks that had already been laid.

'No not there!' Jessie had exclaimed at Barry who was now trying to take another trowel full from the metal bucket and was dropping it all over his new white socks and sandals.

'Oh no you don't my son!' he had said as he hastily rescued the trowel and restrained Barry who was attempting to run off with it. Peeved at being thwarted, Barry had firmly folded his arms and looked daggers at his parents. They had all laughed at this antic and then Laughton had given the trowel to Jessie and she with the help of Humphrey placed the stone between the bricks where a space had been left for it. Then taking his hand in hers she had put them on the stone together and with all her children around her now had simply said 'Palmers Hill.' He knew from her tone what was in her mind. She would make a home here for them all; the way she had at 'The Cottage' and then at 'Maryknowle'. Jessie loved life but she loved her home even more. For her it would be a dream come true once Palmers Hill was complete.

After the laying of the stone they had wandered over to where the footings had been laid for his stabling. There would be two stables side by side and a tack room to accommodate his hunter with room for another horse if either of the boys showed an aptitude for riding. The boys had run off into the thicker woodland where he eventually planned to have a rifle range. They had all met up again to return home by the rickety stile which led back into Brake Lane. There would have to be a wooden gate there when it was all finished. They had then turned right and re-traced their steps back along the lane to where he had parked the car by what would become the main entrance. Although the stone pyramid capped pillars had not yet been built to mark the entrance to the driveway he could see them in his mind's eye. But the name was already there, marked in paint on the temporary gate, 'Palmers Hill'. No doubt Grooms had put that there to ensure tradesmen were able to find the site easily.

Following that momentous day the house came on in leaps and bounds. So did the bills and soon the mounting costs were over his budget. He recalled how Joe Brayne and Humphrey Groom had met him to discuss costs on site. He had laid the problem quickly at their feet.

'Gentlemen, this is all costing me too much. I will not be able to finish Palmers Hill unless you can save me some money. We are already over the original costs for where we have reached.'

'But Mr Goodwin,' said Joe, 'You must remember that we have already saved money on the foundations. Mr Groom wanted to use semi-engineering bricks below ground but when they were costed out you rejected that idea; that actually saved you several hundred pounds in materials and labour.'

'Were those the dark red bricks you showed me?' he had asked.

'Yes the ones which don't absorb much water.'

'Well yes, I do remember that conversation but we are still over budget!'

'If you recall we had to put in some reinforcement to the foundations over the far side of the house where the soil was less solid; that increased the costs there and that was totally unforeseeable.'

'Well how are you going to save me some money now!' he recalled himself saying with some desperation.

The architect had exchanged a knowing glance with the builder. There was a moment's hesitation.

'I suppose we could use breeze blocks for some of the non-supporting internal walls.' rejoined Joe, 'though I personally don't like them much, it would undoubtedly bring the cost down. They're much cheaper than the common bricks we'd planned to use and don't take up so much of the bricklayers time so there would be a big labour saving there as well.'

'I would prefer to use the specified brick,' said Humphrey rather dogmatically.

'Have you ordered those yet from Himley?' asked Joe.

'No, Alan Jones was going to order them next week. We will be needing them the week after.'

'So we haven't incurred any purchase cost yet?'

'No and I could get breeze blocks just as easily; probably more easily, I suppose.'

Laughton had noticed the note of reluctance in his voice but was enthusiastic to save money. He was not to be put off.

'In that case what can you both save me?' he had interjected.

It was Humphrey who had answered. 'I would think probably two hundred pounds, maybe a bit more.'

'Then lets do it shall we!'

There had been similar discussions later but generally after that first exchange about costs somehow both his architect and builder had managed to work closer to the budget than before.

Within a month they were at first floor level, gaps having been left for the windows and external doors with the brickwork carrying on above concrete lintels. Wooden scaffolding lashed together with rope and heavily populated by planking was now being installed. The clean lines of the house were then lost to view and would not be seen again until the house was finished. The ground sub-floor meanwhile had gone in; hardcore with a weak mix of concrete screed over it. A whole honeycomb of low sleeper walls had been constructed above it. After that the carpenters had come in to fix cross timbers which would support the suspended floors. All the internal walls rose too and at first floor level the pine joists went in ready for its flooring to be laid later.

After that it was not many weeks before the building reached roof level. The lorry was now making daily trips arriving with window frames and doors manufactured by the joiners back at Grooms yard in Worcester. Back and forth it went until they were all neatly stacked by the sheds and covered with tarpaulins ready to be fitted in all the many gaps left for them by the wet trades.

Then came the roof with its trusses, joining purlins and rafters. His memory went immediately to the time that the specialist tilers brought in by Grooms were laying the sarking felt on top of the rafters. The whole house was encompassed in scaffolding and there were various access ladders lashed to prevent slippage. It was towards the end of the summer. The days were shortening and they had just returned from a week's holiday at his father-in-law's holiday place, 'Surf Point' at Rhosneiger. It was a warm dry day. He had gone up to talk to Alan and see for himself what had been happening whilst they had been away. Jessie had had enough of the boys and was wishing them back at school. Betty was in a mood because she had not had whatever it was she wanted that day. So he had taken the boys with him. On arrival as was their wont they had gone off to play in the woodland. He had been talking to Alan in his office. They were about finished when Mac called to them from outside the door.

'Father, Barry is up on the scaffolding and I don't think he can get down!'

'Show me where he is Mac.' Laughton and Alan had rushed outside.

'There, up there.' Mac pointed and looking up Laughton had seen Barry right on the edge of the roof near the toe boards swinging on one of the inner handrails.

He had shouted, 'Stop doing that this instant Barry and stand still!' Barry had done as he was told.

'Don't move, just stay there. I will come and get you.' he had called commandingly to his youngest son. What on earth was he doing up there? Quickly he had climbed up the ladder. A minute or so later he reached Barry who seemed somewhat nonchalant as to what all the fuss was about. He recalled he had said nothing at that time but guided Barry so he descended backwards down the ladder. Back on the ground he berated him.

'I have told you before you are not to climb up any of the ladders.'

'I know Father but there was this tortoiseshell butterfly I saw high up on the scaffolding so I went after it. I need one to pin in my collection for school.'

'Come on, you did not need to be swinging on that handrail to swot a butterfly!'

'No but it was there so I did. I really enjoyed being up there. I wasn't in the least bit frightened you know?'

'And what if you had fallen?'

'But I didn't did I!' came the rather truculent retort.

Not wasting breath on a further remark Laughton had reflected that that was not the first time he had noticed the difference between his two sons. Mac calm, collected and meticulously sensible; grown-up before his time; Barry full of effervescent zest and go; rather reckless at times. He had thought how like himself, when young and had admired the boy's pluck.

'Well you had better not say anything to your mother when we get home.' he had said to both of them in the car as they drove back to Clent. Neither did any of them mention what had happened that day until years later when it could matter no more!

Thousands of tiles now arrived on site from the same manufacturers near Dudley who had produced the facing bricks. The tilers started at the eaves and gradually worked their way up the roof to the ridge nailing the tiles to the battens which had been laid the length of the roof across the rafters on top of the sarking felt. Plumbers arrived to beat out and marry the lead flashing to the contours of the roof around the chimney stack and in the valleys. At last the ridge tiles were cemented into place and the roof was complete.

He recalled that particular week for after a long and comparatively dry summer there had been a violent thunderstorm which had started whilst he was visiting the site on his own at the end of a working day. A strike of lightning simultaneous with a tumultuous clap of thunder had told him that the storm was immediately overhead. He recalled being particularly glad he had taken the advice of Joe Brayne and had those copper lightening strips fitted to the four chimney stacks. He had been forced to take shelter within the new house whose windows were now glazed and through which he had watched the drenched soil around the house turn to mud until the sun had briefly shone again to form a complete rainbow against the thunderous blue of the sky.

Inside the house the floors were now laid but not yet fixed; oak on the ground floor and softwood on the first floor and over the garage. Plasterers working on protective tarpaulins were busy finishing off the last of the internal walls. Their work had been preceded by the electrician doing his first fix. Rubber covered wires ran it seemed at one stage almost everywhere but now appeared only as if to surprise one, out of the newly plastered walls at all levels, to eventually supply switches; wall and ceiling lights and sockets.

He recalled that when he had been concerned about the mess left by the plasterers, Alan had told him that the floor timbers would be finally turned and fixed and the staircases put in once they had finished; that way the wood would not be damaged. Finally, the skirting boards, architraves and window sills were fixed into place; the doors were hung. The various white baths and sinks with their chrome taps he and Jessie had chosen were in. It had seemed to him that the whole house had started to take on a character of its own; friendly and peaceful it felt a safe haven to which he would be able to return time and again from the stormy commercial world of selling cars.

Chapter 13

PUBLIC SCHOOL FOR THE 'BOYS'

As the boys grew up and became young men he had realized that both of them were naturals with engines and all things mechanical. He had added the Shed to Palmers Hill down by the Stables soon after Mac had joined Shrewsbury School following The Wells House. He had resigned himself by then to the fact that his boys' talent was practical not academic and that they needed somewhere in the holidays to indulge their passion for engines. The Shed had at last solved the problem of engines and bits of engines and oily rags being left all over the pristine clean garage where he kept the cars!

Mac at Shrewsbury School had been placed in Rigg House where even his housemaster, Philip Ashurst, despite thirty years experience of teaching, was unable to produce anything but mediocrity from him! Strange how neither boy had wanted to be at the same school. They said they had had enough of that at The Wells House. Each of them had made various juvenile excuses but he had felt that at the bottom of it all was the fact each had thought it cramped their style!

So Barry had gone to Bryanston School in Dorset instead of Shrewsbury. There on the outskirts of Blandford Forum amongst rolling country he had found his métier. Sport! He had been just fourteen. It was 1931. Laughton could still visualize that half mile long dark leafy driveway up from the main road to the school.

In his three years at Bryanston Barry had come of age. He was in Hardy House, named after Thomas Hardy whose books Jessie was always reading. His housemaster, Harry Green, who had been with the school since its foundation in 1928 and himself a sports fanatic, had immediately encouraged Barry's prowess on the playing field and in the swimming pool. Barry seemed to play rugby for his house or school daily!

As an exceptional swimmer he was also in the School's diving and water polo teams. His spasmodic and badly spelt letters used to be full of it. First for this and first for that! He had even rowed for a while and been in the 'B' Eight who beat the school's 'A' crew by a third of a length in what had been a hard fought touch and go race. Laughton and Jessie had stood on the side of the river and cheered him on as Barry had stroked his boat to glory!

It was during one of the boys' summer holidays when he had engaged a firm to build the swimming pool at Palmers Hill as he had promised. A hard tennis court had already been constructed as had been the shooting range where he himself had practiced regularly. He had contacted Humphrey Groom who was by then something of a friend. Humphrey had said that the Groom expertise did not really stretch to building tiled swimming pools! He had suggested that Laughton should employ a specialist firm but had not been able to recommend any particular one.

He could not recall now who had suggested Wiggins Pools but they had seemed all right and their quote had been perfectly reasonable. In fact theirs had been the middle quote out of the three he had obtained. But they were slow at starting and then it seemed, even slower excavating the ground out at the back of Palmers Hill, on the house side of the tennis court. Really slow!

During that long school holiday most of the time Mac and Barry were either busy with engines in the Shed or out with their pals. They had always been very popular with their own age group and were often invited to parties. Both girls and boys used to enjoy their company. Barry was beginning to develop into quite a dashing young man with his blonde hair and patrician looks. It seemed that he had particularly taken to the company of Lavinia, Cobham's daughter. She was a frequent visitor to Palmers Hill and would travel with the family sometimes when they paid visits to the hill climb at Shelsley Walsh. Whether there was anything in it not even Jessie had discovered and he certainly had never been told. They had seemed more than very close friends but Barry always kept those sort of matters very private whereas Mac had always wanted to be completely open with him. With Barry it had always been better not to pry as he had a fiery temper!

Lavinia had played a more obvious part in the family however when Betty was in her late teens. Lavinia had rather taken her under her wing. He recalled how they used to ride with him in the early morning and on occasions the two of them used to visit local racing establishments. They also liked accompanying Lavinia's father, a keen follower of the horses, on trips to local racecourses.

Indeed he had a framed photograph of them in his Gun Room standing side by side in the enclosure at the 1938 Gold Cup Meeting at Cheltenham studying the list of runners. The photograph had been taken by one of the Daily Sketch photographers and later reproduced in some women's fashion magazine. It must have been very cold that day. Both of them had their hoods up and been wearing gloves. Betty's hands were covered with those ghastly mock leopard skin gauntlets that she had bought at Marshall and Snelgrove's during an earlier shopping expedition with Jessie to Birmingham. He had always detested them and so she had never worn them when out with her parents.

But on that occasion they had been captured on camera, Lavinia wearing a black and white checked suit with a fox fur hat and his daughter, her camel coat.

How pretty they had both looked. He knew they used to bet on horses, the names of which came as tips from some of the stable lads up at Hagley Hall. Only on that March day at Cheltenham did he recall them ever winning any serious money though!

Golden Miller had won the race so many times in previous years and was a hot favourite to win yet again despite being twelve years old. His odds had been short. The big money had gone on him in the betting. Inspired by her two older brothers telling her about the Morse Code they had been learning in the Auxiliary Air Force, Betty had ignored the advice of the touts and had backed the horse called 'Morse Code'. She had encouraged Lavinia to do likewise.

Laughton imagined the scene when they had gone along the line of on-course bookies to find the best odds so each of them could put a couple of quid on Morse Code. At fifty to one it had just beaten off Golden Miller at the finish after three miles of hard pressed gallop. They had each won £100! Cobham had dropped Betty off at Palmers Hill late that evening before returning to Hagley Hall with Lavinia. Betty was giggly and plainly they had all been having a drink or two to celebrate! Her pockets were still stuffed with wads of notes!

Now though the memory of the swimming pool returned. Mac and Barry had wanted to enjoy that hot summer in a tiled pool. They had become frustrated by the fact the builders kept going off on other jobs and not attending to the pool at Palmers Hill. They had not responded positively to Laughton telling them to be more patient. Eventually they had taken matters into their own hands.

Simon Thursley was a close friend of Mac's at that time. He was employed to lay charges at a local quarry at Seisdon near Wolverhampton. He was often at Palmers Hill playing tennis with Mac. Laughton had noticed his backhand was particularly powerful when he had played doubles matches with Barry against Mac and Simon. Laughton recalled how he and Jessie had been sitting relaxing in the snug at the front of the house totally unaware of what was going on outside. There had been an almighty blast and then the rear windows had rattled as they were pelted with earth and debris.

'What the hell was that?' he had exclaimed as he put out his cigarette, leapt to his feet, jammed on his outdoor shoes and hurried to the back door to find out. He feared some major catastrophe had occurred down at the Shed. Instead when he had stepped out of the yard at the rear of the house he had found the boys looking rather dazed and shell shocked together with a huge crater that had been blown out by the explosion. The hole started by the contractors was now big enough for a swimming pool and a half! Earth, stones and other remains including some of Jessie's treasured rose bushes were scattered over an area of at least a hundred feet! Fortunately both boys were still alive!

When he examined the back of Palmers Hill he found that even some of the windows had been cracked by the force of the blast. He had the story out of young Mac and Barry in an instant. Mac had persuaded Simon to provide enough gelignite and fuses to blow a big enough hole for the swimming pool in one go! Simon had instructed them how to lay the charges with the fuses but the charges had gone off earlier than expected!

Apparently Mac and Simon were about the same build and Simon needed an evening suit so he could take his latest girlfriend to a local dinner dance. In exchange for explosives Mac had lent him his black tie!

Laughton recalled how furious he had felt despite his initial concern. Indeed it was only the intervention of Jessie who had followed him outside which prevented him from laying hands on Mac and Barry despite their size! As it was he had hardly spoken to them for twenty four hours afterwards and had made them clear up the mess they had made of the garden. Secretly though, he could not but admire their initiative and yes, the pool had indeed been finished much faster than had been anticipated. Certainly, all the family had been able to bathe in it before the season had passed!

Chapter 14

NELL AND MAC

Mac had met Nell at a party in Alcester. It must have been at least four years probably longer after Mac had started working with him at the garage. Nell had been only eighteen Mac, twenty three. By the time they met, Mac had been around with several girlfriends but none of them lasted as Nell had done. Indeed many of them had lasted no longer than a few days or weeks and were never introduced to the parents save by name in passing conversation.

When Laughton first met Nell he had immediately liked her. Petite, blonde and very pretty she had an effervescent nature which infected all those around her with her good humour. Nothing ever seemed to bother her. Maybe that was because she was the daughter of an Earl or maybe it was the confidence of youth. Her upbringing at Overton Hall near Alcester was very silver spoon with education at Roedean before finishing school in Switzerland.

Somewhere amongst all that superiority, surprisingly she had learnt to cook and made the most marvellous chocolate cakes. Laughton recalled the one she had made for Mac's twenty-fifth birthday in December 1939. Adorned with lit candles she had carried it from the kitchen into the darkened drawing room at Palmers Hill to the accompaniment of 'Happy Birthday' before presenting it as a surprise to Mac with a kiss!

Most of the family and many of Mac's friends all in service uniform had been there that night drinking him dry of Champagne. What a happy night that had been and how distant the War had seemed despite the uniforms. Mac's twenty-first at Palmers Hill had been up until then the jolliest party. Laughton recalled that it had been during that earlier party that he and Jessie had given him his Rolex wristwatch with the brown leather strap. It had been a generous present even by their standards but what pleasure they had received. Mac had been completely overwhelmed and had spontaneously reached out and had hugged him and then kissed his mother. He was a very affectionate boy. Barry was much more detached and although the girls flocked round him Laughton had always had the impression that he preferred fast cars and aircraft to fast women!

Mac was often at Overton Hall after he had met Nell. In fact the two of them were inseparable and went everywhere together. Often Nell would drive over to see them at Palmers Hill or borrow one of Felix's horses to go riding with Mac. They seemed to spend every evening together out at parties and dances. One morning rather earlier than normal he recalled going downstairs to get a cup of tea as he couldn't sleep only to meet Mac creeping upstairs in his black tie just back from a night out with Nell! Mac had joined him for his tea and told him some cock and bull story of getting lost coming back to Palmers Hill. Laughton had simply patted him on the back and said 'I remember just how easy it is to get lost at your age!' and nothing further had been said!

As time passed and the relationship continued he and Jessie had suspected that Mac and Nell were contemplating marriage although suddenly that had seemed a more distant prospect once War had been declared.

The memory suddenly recalled that day when Mac had telephoned him from Overton Hall. Mac had flown the Tiger Moth from Palmers Hill over to Alcester to see Nell for tea. He had landed in one of the fenced fields in the grounds. Apparently according to Mac he had been enjoying a rather lavish tea with Nell and her family when the butler had entered the room. In a rather formal and ponderous manner he had announced to Nell, 'My lady, the cows are eating Mr. Goodwin's aeroplane!'

In disbelief Mac and Nell had run out to see what on earth had been happening. Some cows had been let into the field after Mac's arrival and they had been intrigued by the presence in their field of the aeroplane. They had gone over and started to lick the wings and fuselage with their thick rubbery tongues. Obviously they had found the taste of the dope on the canvas not only to their liking but also stimulating! By the time Mac and Nell reached them, the cows were quite skittish on dope!

Unfortunately the wings had been reduced to a decidedly soggy state. Hence the telephone call to him at the garage from Mac to explain what had happened and asking for a lorry to be dispatched to transport it back to Palmers Hill. Laughton had dined out on that story for months until Jessie had told him 'enough is enough!' He could hear her voice now.

Nell also had come with them up to Rhosneiger on a couple of occasions when they went to 'The Dunes'. The family had always enjoyed their holidays on Anglesey. In the early years they had always stayed at 'Surf Point' which his father in law had built earlier and which was known locally and affectionately as 'Sausage Castle'. A huge rambling edifice the house commanded the golden sands which lay beyond it. The views from inside towards the sea itself were stunning. Access to the sand was so easy for the children. All they had to do was to walk out of the side door and they were there! Hours of their holiday childhood were spent on that beach building sand castles with moats and stream systems for the sea to invade as the tide came in. Their gaiety and laughter sounded in his mind even now. Such happy days those had been.

After Charles Henry died in 1922 his wife Amy hardly ventured up to Anglesey and 'Surf Point' deteriorated; its furnishing became faded splendour. He and Jessie had wanted their own place in Rhosneiger but something more to their liking. When 'The Dunes' had come up for sale in 1928 just beyond the main entrance to 'Surf Point' they had gone to look at it. It was an ancient solid stone house several centuries old but with spacious and modernized accommodation. The price in Anglesey was cheap compared with prices back in Hagley and they had immediately put an offer in below the asking price.

Over a month had passed and then suddenly a letter had arrived from the estate agents to say that the previous owner had died and that his estate had decided to accept Laughton's offer. The result was that many of their summer holidays thereafter had been at 'The Dunes' and both as children and teenagers the boys had loved the place. It was such a peaceful haven near the sea where you could get out of the wind to sunbathe. On hot summer's nights as you lay in bed with the windows wide open the air was like a soft balm and you could fall asleep to the sound of the waves lapping at the shore as the tide slipped in.

He and Jessie had enjoyed having Nell with them at the Dunes. She never put on any pretence and played her part in helping Jessie and keeping them all entertained with her amusing anecdotes. He and Jessie hoped that eventually she would become their daughter in law once the war was over.

Chapter 15

SHELSLEY WALSH – A FIRST RUN

Barry had always loved speed. Anything which went fast in the air or on the ground! He used to like it when Laughton had taken him out as a young boy and driven at 70 mph which was about the safe top limit his Hudson could manage! When at last Barry had flown Jack's plane for the first time solo aged sixteen his reckless enthusiasm had come to the fore more than ever before! Laughton was by then flying himself and owned a single-seater biplane which he flew from the field at the back of Palmers Hill. After the boys had both learnt to fly with Jack he had allowed them to fly it when he was around. Jessie had told him relatively recently that at least once Barry had flown it when he wasn't!

On that occasion she had actually heard the sound of the aeroplane engine being started and had gone outside to investigate as she knew Barry had some friends with him that day. They had been at a loose end, showing the usual boredom of teenagers with not enough to do! After feeding them with freshly cooked buns and mugs of tea, she had shooed them from her kitchen and seen them through the kitchen window wandering off towards the Shed.

Once outside she could see that they were all in the field. As she had walked over to remonstrate with Barry for starting up his father's aeroplane she was horrified to see it taxi and take off. Even before she reached the field he had turned the aeroplane and brought it in a low pass just above his friends' heads. He was showing off but although cross she could not help being impressed by his obvious flying skills as she saw him flying over the neighbouring fields of golden barley, almost ready for Felix to harvest.

Barry meanwhile seemed to be coming in to land. Perhaps he had spotted her in the field. She was terrified that he would crash but he set it down with expert ease stopping, she noticed, exactly where the wheels used to rest when Laughton himself used it. She had not known he could be so devious! He had then pushed himself up from the cockpit and leapt down from the side before coming over to her looking rather sheepish.

'You silly boy!' she had reacted angrily to him probably as much out of anxiety as from anger itself, 'You could have got yourself killed just then.

'Well I didn't did I. I do know how to fly you know mother!' he had rejoined defiantly as Jessie packed his friends off and ordered him to return to the house 'Don't tell father I have been flying it will you?' he had then begged and Jessie had promised she wouldn't provided he did not fly again without his father being there.

Suddenly, those thoughts stimulated another memory. Another of Barry's early mechanized adventures. He supposed Barry must have been over the age to drive with a proper licence but then he could not be sure as he had let the boys drive cars up and down the drive at Palmers Hill and even along Brake Lane for as long as he could remember.

But this memory related to a lorry! He had brought a chassis on wheels down from the works for the boys to strip and put together to learn from it. It still had its driver's seat, braking system and steering mechanism intact but without an engine it was going nowhere! The boys must have been in their mid-teens for Mac had recently discovered girls so that for a time he was distracted somewhat. So it was Barry who had spent most time on it; not only putting it back together but adapting it for his own purposes!

It was P.C. John Sutcliffe who had eventually told him about what had happened. Laughton had known that an old aero-engine abandoned by Uncle Jack had found its way to the Shed. Barry had come up with a harebrained scheme of using it to power the old lorry. Unbeknown to Laughton at the time, this part he had managed by bolting the engine down onto the rear of the chassis. The engine was now fixed so it could propel the chassis forward and he would be able to drive it using the existing steering and brakes. Having achieved that, of course, the temptation had been to try it out!

Barry somehow had managed to get the chassis and its extra payload over to the hill in Hoarstone Lane that ran past Bridewell Cottage in Bewdley just up from the River Severn. Laughton had purchased the property as a weekend retreat for the family a few years before and he understood how Barry would have chosen the hill for his experiment. It was a challenging hill not unlike one that would have been ideal for speed hill climbing!

Barry had placed a number of his young friends as look outs at strategic points up the long narrow twisting corners of the hill. He would have started up the aero engine by swinging the propeller. What speed it would have been able to muster for the chassis he dreaded to think but with the propeller whirling no doubt on full throttle Barry had raced the lorry up the hill timing it on a stopwatch he had acquired.

All went reasonably well on the first run. On the second or third run however, disaster had struck as a tractor towing a trailer full of manure had turned right out of Hoarstone Manor Farm and directly into Barry's path. Barry had tried desperately to avoid it but had collided with the trailer and that night Laughton recalled when he had returned to Palmers Hill he had still stunk of manure!

The farmer who Laughton knew vaguely had been well within his rights to complain about Barry's outrageous, if not thoroughly dangerous behaviour, on the public highway. Fortunately, the trailer was not badly damaged but it had taken a visit from Laughton to him and payment for the repairs before the farmer was suitably mollified.

P.C. Sutcliffe was ironically much more amenable. He had teenage boys himself and had been quite amused by Barry's 'high jinks' as he had called them. Fortunately as all had been made right by Laughton, there was in the end no prosecution for having no insurance, or for racing on the public highway or any other of the many offences that Barry seemed to have committed! The chassis was written off and Barry was grounded!

Thinking back now Barry's more adult attempts at motor sport had started in earnest just after he had left Bryanston when Uncle Jack had bought that two seater TT Replica with the 1500cc Meadows engine for him and Barry to drive. What was the registration? Oh yes he could still remember it, MV2013! It was already three years old by the time Jack got his hands on it. Jack had known Roy Eccles who owned it and who had raced it on the Hill at Shelsley.

Jack had bought it after Barry's escapade with the lorry saying it was to keep him out of trouble! It must have been in about 1935. Jack in his opinion had always been far too indulgent with both his nephews; buying that horse for Mac and now this car for Barry. He supposed he had been rather jealous at the close rapport Jack had always had with the boys from when they were quite small.

In fairness to Jack he had asked Laughton whether he would mind him buying the car. Laughton had felt obliged to say 'no he didn't' for after all he had been an enthusiastic hill climber himself at Shelsley until not too long before! Indeed he had even managed to come second in the Garvagh Cup in his Chrysler back in 1928.

Barry had tried out the car along Brake Lane and also taken it up Hoarstone Lane where he had taken the chassis but this time he had used more spotters. He had also had the sense to use that part of the hill that lay beyond Hoarstone Farm!

He and Uncle Jack had also taken it over to Madresfield in a furniture van and competed a few times there and at other events around the Midlands in which his Class had comprised just a few cars, usually about nine or ten. Laughton had gone to watch on a number of occasions and had been impressed by Barry's obvious feel for the car although he was still very inexperienced.

His familiarization with the car and that experience gained over the summer of 1935 had placed him in a position of being able to contemplate an entry to Shelsley the following year. Although Jack had said that he would be driving the car as well Laughton had seen no sign of him driving it in competition in those early days. Jack had simply been encouraging Barry to 'go for it!'

In September 1935 Barry had come with him and Jessie to the September meeting at Shelsley so that he could watch his hero Raymond Mays. Mays driving his two litre ERA did not disappoint him and made the fastest time of that day in 39.6 seconds. It was the last meeting before the Midland Automobile Club who ran the events at Shelsley sub-divided their pure speed events into a simple two classes 'supercharged' and 'unsupercharged'.

He recalled walking up the hill to the right of the course with his younger son as spectators that day. Barry was very excited by the possibility of competing at such a famous venue next season. Laughton had explained to him how the course panned out as you went up the one thousand yard Hill with its one in nine average gradient, and the lines he should take at each of the bends.

The twelve foot track which originally had been simply a bridle path was now tarmacadam. Getting a good start without too much wheel spin was important. Then came the first left hand bend known as Kennel Bend, before one accelerated up and through the Crossing, another bend to the left but a more gradual one. Quickly there followed two more bends, the first known as the Bottom 'S', a tight left hander and then shortly after that the Top 'S' which swung you ninety degrees to the right and onto the Straight that led you to the Finish. As they stood on the elevated bank to the right of the Bottom 'S', Barry had watched intently as various cars had swept past them to brake for their entry to the bend.

It was in the spring of the following year that Barry had had his first runs up the Hill at the MAC's first meeting in the May of 1936. On the back of his limited experience he was delighted that his entry for the 1500cc unsupercharged Class had been accepted. He would have just turned nineteen. The rest of the family had come to watch. On Practice Day Barry had signed on and had the car passed by the scrutineers. The official ticket had been tied on a length of string to the seat so it was to hand to show the Paddock marshalls or the start line marshalls before any of his runs.

Barry had been highly excited about competing at what was after all a national event with no less than sixteen cars in his Class alone. Doing well was obviously important to him. Jack Humphreys who had been recruited by Laughton to help prepare the car was on hand to help Barry be ready. Jack had had considerable experience with other racers on the Hill but as he had worked for Laughton for as long as he could remember and had known Barry since he was a child, his loyalty had meant that he had now concentrated his effort on them alone.

At the end of the Practice Day after his two runs Barry was really pleased to be third quickest in his Class. Back at Palmers Hill that evening he had analyzed his approach to the Hill with his father. Laughton could not temper Barry's excitement for the morrow or get him to see the dangers of going flat out through that second corner, the Crossing. Barry made it quite clear that he intended to really push the car through the Crossing in Saturday's runs having eased off a tad in the preliminary runs that day.

The next day is fortunately fine and when they arrive at Shelsley for Race Day the track is dry and the forecast for once does not feature rain! He feared that Barry was over-confident but then had he not been like that himself! He said said nothing.

The first run puts Barry fourth in his Class but the competitors are so close that Barry reckons a good second run could put him first. He is determined to show he has the guts to take the Crossing without lifting his right foot!

With Barry in line waiting to reach the Start he and Jessie walk up to the Crossing to watch looking back down the track. Barry's run is next. They hear the Frazer-Nash come up from the start with the engine sounding like the tearing of calico as Barry keeps the revs at maximum torque. Here he comes! Undoubtedly, he is really trying but he cannot take this corner at that speed. 'Take your foot off a bit' Laughton had shouted as if Barry could have heard and responded. As it was the words went to the wind and Barry pressed on recklessly, the confidence of youth overriding inexperience!

His turn in is too aggressive. He is just past the apex. Perhaps he will still get away with it! No, the Nash's tail is sliding too far out to the right hand side. It kisses the bank in front of us. The front of the car is now unbalanced and turns into the bank. Velocity causes it to cartwheel throwing Barry onto the road! The car comes to rest further up the track minus its front right wheel which has been torn off and lazily rolls a few yards back down the course towards the Start before tipping over and lying in the middle of the track.

Jessie has her hands momentarily over her face in stark horror. It was then as much as he could do to prevent her from running out onto the track to Barry who remained motionless on the tarmac. Marshalls had already reached him and were covering him with warm blankets. The ambulance was being driven up to the accident from where it was parked at the Kennel. Oh good, the doctor is there now and checking him over. The black uniformed St. John's ambulance men lift him carefully onto a stretcher and load him into the ambulance.

Jessie and he quickly run back to the medical room. By the time they get there Barry is already sitting up and the nursing attendant has a cup of tea ready to hand to him. No doubt it has some sugar in it! Barry hates sweet tea!

The doctor, Dr. Mortimer, is examining his chest. Barry is bleeding from abrasions on his body, arms and knees but is still completely winded and is finding it very difficult to catch his breath.

'Is he all right?' Laughton asks.

Before the doctor can remove his stethoscope from his ears Barry still slightly gasping for breath and somewhat confused manages to answer for him.

'I'll be fine in a mo ...... you can stop worrying ...... just a few cuts and grazes will they let me go again? ...... what do you think?'

Dr. Mortimer looks at his young patient quizzically over his half rimmed gold spectacles.

'Your hill climbing is over for today Barry. Your breathing is only just coming back to normal. Your chest took a big impact when you were thrown out. You are not fit to drive again today.'

'And the car is wrecked so you won't be driving it again for sometime let alone today! I told you, you had to lay off a bit on that bend. Why do you always think you can get away with it?' Laughton adds thinking of the expense of re-building the car.

'Because I live a charmed life!' Barry replies audaciously with a laugh and an engaging smile that reaps immediate forgiveness for the havoc he had just caused his parents emotions and pocket!

Back in the Paddock Jack Humphreys is helping the marshalls bring back the Frazer-Nash. The car looks in a sorry state, pretty badly dented and scraped.

'How is he Mr. Laughton?' Jack asks looking most concerned.

'Pretty chirpy considering, Jack. Probably more anxious about the car than himself. What about the car, what do you think? Looks badly mangled to me.'

'Oh don't worry about the car Mr. Laughton it's only beaten aluminum! I will soon have that sorted once we get it back to Palmers Hill but I may need to take some parts back to the works to machine new ones.'

A quarter of an hour later Dr. Mortimer pronounced that Barry was fit to travel. His various superficial cuts and abrasions had been treated. They had taken him back to Palmers Hill with him moaning en route that he had only wanted to win his Class! Laughton had reassured him telling him that there would be other opportunities.

Well that was how it all had started at Shelsley. Despite the accident he had thought Barry had shown early promise as a hill climber but would be better once he had had a couple of successful seasons behind him. Indeed in September 1936 although only taking part for the second time at Shelsley Barry had managed to win his unsupercharged Class with a time of 48.38 seconds.

Uncle Jack had at last started to drive himself and had been rather taken by the sport. He had also been enthusiastic enough about Barry's potential to sell the TT Replica and buy another 1500cc Frazer-Nash, this one being a single seater supercharged model. Barry's times for the Hill of course had immediately improved and by the spring of 1938 he was beginning to close down on the challenge of beating 40 seconds. In the Spring Meeting in 1938 he was down to about 42.6 when he, and Fane and Ansell had won the team Fray Challenge Trophy for the MAC team.

Indeed Jack Humphreys had told him that in one of the preliminary runs on Practice Day Barry had even beaten the record for the Hill but the marshalls had said that the timing mechanism had not functioned properly for some reason and so the time was not accepted. Barry had been terribly disappointed but had bounced back with a determination that he would be up there with Mays and Fane exchanging the record with them very soon.

Chapter 16

SHELSLEY WALSH 1938

Laughton recalled they had woken early that September morning with sunshine pouring into their bedroom. Opening the window to clear the tang of sleep that pervaded the room he had realised that the air was crisp with an icy edge of winter looming about it. The driveway was dry. It was going to be a very good day for Barry's hill climb at Shelsley.

He had stood there for a moment before going to shave readying himself for the day. Palmers Hill as ever retained its magic. The leaves in the woodland adjoining the drive where Mac and Barry used to play as youngsters were changing colour. The green luxuriant leaves of summer were being replaced by those soft autumnal beiges and browns that burnished by sunlight made them look like luxurious velvet. The lawn was still growing but the gardeners were gradually putting the garden to bed as winter approached. There was a still a hint of burnt wood on the air from the fire they had been burning yesterday on the edge of the woodland at the rear of Palmers Hill.

Something nostalgic he had always thought at this time of year about the smell of wood smoke. It spoke of long days of physical work in the garden often on a Sunday followed by the cleansing of a fire over which one could enjoy a pipe and idly muse about the week ahead. Yet there was still much colour provided within the rose garden and from the purple dahlias that Jessie so liked and he had so detested but managed to overlook! It was even worse when she insisted on cutting them for floral arrangements within the house itself! He had banished them from the Gun Room.

Finishing his dressing he had gone downstairs. Max Hoffman who was staying with them would be coming with them in Laughton's new Buick to watch Barry compete on the Hill. He had met Max about four years before when he had been invited by Max's father to watch Max compete at the Swiss Grand Prix at Bremgarten driving his own Alfa Romeo. His father, Ernst, was a wealthy industrialist whose interest in racing cars had been fuelled in middle age like Laughton's own by his son's interest. Max also competed in hill climbs. He would be competing today but for a serious leg injury suffered as a result of an accident earlier that year competing in the European Hill Climbing Championship.

Max was already in the dining room having had breakfast and was talking to Jessie. The 'boys' were nowhere to be seen. It turned out that Barry had already left.

'Sorry I am late,' he had proffered but the other two had ignored him and carried on talking about slugs. Jessie was apparently explaining why the vegetable plot was looking so decidedly unproductive. The slugs were endemic and had played havoc with her vegetables this year. He had sat down having collected a glass of fresh squeezed orange juice and a large cup of fresh coffee from the sideboard where Gladys had laid them.

'Will you be riding with me this morning, Max?' he had asked as Max returned to the table with a cup of coffee to join him. 'Felix said you could borrow his chestnut if you wanted a ride.' Max patted his injured leg.

'I not ride with this yet Laughton,' Max had said in his slightly guttural Germanic tone, 'I vould 'ope you forgive me not to ride this morning!'

He had been disappointed. Max was not so lively as he had been when they had first met and he had seen him unsuccessfully compete against the Auto Union Silver Arrows at Bremgarten that year when Hans Stuck had won. True Max had suffered this leg injury earlier in the year but it was strange how some people changed so fundamentally in such a short time.

Laughton sitting in the glade coughed and laughed hollowly at the thought. He himself had now lost the will to live and he was condemning Max just for becoming a bit older! But Max was still only twenty-nine then!

Max was due to compete in a few days time in the postponed British Grand Prix. He had been expected to come to stay with his father but Ernst was then too busy, so Max had come alone. Perhaps the pressure of getting fit enough again to drive the Grand Prix without being able to practise in the meantime was what had been preying on his mind. He nevertheless seemed more careworn than when he had visited Palmers Hill with his father the previous year.

Laughton recalled finishing his breakfast and grabbing his riding jacket and hat. He had strode across the back lawn past the swimming pool in good humour to collect his fifteen hand hunter, Evershed, from the stable at the bottom of the garden where Ivy, the stable maid, had just finished grooming him. He had called him 'Evershed' because when first he had bought him to ride, the horse had shown an awful tendency to shy at fences and pitch his rider, which was usually himself, over his head! But he had managed to train him out of doing that and by then he would jump almost any five bar gate or field hedgerow.

On that morning he had thrown his saddle across Evershed's back and watching that the horse played no tricks by expanding his stomach he had pulled the girth strap comfortably tight to fasten it whilst Ivy strapped on the bridle and reins. Then putting his right foot in the stirrup whilst Ivy held Evershed's head he had swung his left leg over the horse and mounted. Soon he was down onto Brake Lane then away from Palmers Hill riding across Felix's fields on his morning gallop. Those gallops taken in the early mornings had brought him so much pleasure across the years. They always made him feel exhilarated and full of energy. That day was no exception.

As he approached the stables on his return to Palmers Hill he came across the furniture lorry parked in Brake Lane near the Shed. He left Evershed with Ivy who was cleaning out the stables and changing the straw. Evershed was steaming and needed attention but he trusted Ivy to ensure he was well cared for. Meanwhile he had made his way down to the Shed where he found Jack Humphreys who had the Frazer-Nash on the wagon and was busily collecting up spare tyres and tools he might need at the meeting.

'Morning Mr Laughton,' Jack greeted him rather more curtly than usual. As he responded he looked at his watch and realised that Jack must be running late to get to Shelsley in time for the first eliminating runs as they were now called. He had asked if he could lend a hand but it appeared that Jack had nearly finished his loading with some spare gear chains for the Frazer-Nash and was about to leave.

He had stood there and watched as the big van had set off down the lane leaving exhaust fumes in its wake which had caused him to turn rapidly and head back up to the house. He too needed to get changed and off in the Buick to Shelsley with Jessie and Max. When he went in through the back door he found Jessie in the kitchen preparing the picnic which they always took with them; home cooked ham sandwiches on home baked bread with butter from Holmewood Farm the other side of Hagley; a thermos or two of tea and Jessie's own fruit cake. She was still the love of his life and the centre of the way in which the family operated. She gave him a smile as he passed.

'I am almost ready,' she had said as if he had asked her whether she was or wasn't. He had laughed and gone to quickly change.

When they had arrived at Shelsley they had parked the Buick in the field that was now allocated for spectators cars. He and Max had then unloaded the picnic basket and between them carried it to the Paddock. The Paddock area was so much better than when first he had raced at Shelsley with the Essex in the twenties. A firm surface had replaced the muddy field and the competitors were allocated numbered pits. He and Jessie had found Barry in number 26 on the far side of the Paddock.

Barry and Jack Humphreys were busy working on the super-charged Frazer-Nash. The Frazer-Nash with its allocated competitor's number 19 was under the open line of sheds, the corrugated tin roof of which was held up by simple stanchions of wood to allow free access to the cars they housed. Jack had the engine cover off and he and Barry were both bent over peering at the superchargers at the front. He remembered how exquisite the engineering was to his seasoned eye.

'Problem?' he had asked quizzically after they all had greeted one another and Jessie had kissed her boy.

'Oh no, well I don't think so,' replied Jack, 'we had them out last night to check them over and I am just making sure we tightened them sufficiently; yes, well I think that will do you, young Barry!' he continued as he removed a gleaming chrome spanner from the engine, gave a final rub to the superchargers with the oiled rag he always seemed to have in his hand and stood back from the car admiring its fine lines. For a moment he had stood there with a hand on his lower back. Laughton had realised for the first time that Jack's back was beginning to really trouble him. Then Jack had turned to him and Max.

'Looks well in the new black,' he had said with a smile, at the same time moving as a team with Barry to replace the front engine cover and to buckle it down with the heavy leather straps that held it in place.

Indeed it had 'looked well' to use Jack's artisan phrase. Everything about it, of course, was immaculate.

He had watched as Barry in his flannels, waistcoat, long-sleeved sports shirt with a tie at his neck had grabbed his flying helmet and goggles in his left hand and clambered into the driving seat. Laughton was too tall for the car especially now that they had shortened it by ten inches. He recalled how he had tried to get into it on one occasion before that surgery and had needed help to escape after one of his knees had got stuck! But Barry was shorter and with his youth more agile. He had stepped onto the maroon leather seat and then avoiding holding the sprung steering wheel, he had pushed his legs down into the well of the cockpit.

He had enlisted Max's help and with Jack they had rolled the car just outside the pit onto the tarmac road and then push-started it. The one and a half litre supercharged engine crackled momentarily and then roared into life, settling quickly to a heavy growl. Once warmed they had it back into the pit and Barry had switched off and leapt out to help Jack and Laughton as they put woollen blankets over the bonnet to keep the engine warm. It would soon be Barry's turn for his first run of the day. The loudspeakers were already calling the earlier cars up to the starting line.

Barry was likely to be in the second batch called. Meanwhile Jack Humphreys made last minor adjustments. Then it was time to help again getting the car started. He and Jessie had watched as Barry drove off towards the start and taken his place in the line being directed by the rather officious marshal who was on duty that day. Jack in his clean white overalls he always wore had walked alongside making sure that his young charge reached the line in good order.

Meanwhile he and Jessie had time to walk up the right hand side of the hill to reach Kennel Bend so that they could get a glimpse of Barry shortly after he had started. They did not have to wait long. They soon heard the high pitched wailing of the superchargers as Barry came out of the start area where he had been hidden from their view past 'The Cottage' on his right and then into Kennel. His blonde hair was covered by his flying helmet and his goggles covered his eyes as he worked the car through the bend in what Laughton had thought was an excellent line. Then he was past them in a millisecond and on into the Crossing and hurtling up towards the two esses.

As Barry braked into the Bottom S bend he went too far to the right before turning into the bend momentarily locking a wheel on the loose surface and spoiling his entry to the Bottom S. Laughton knew that small error would cost him some time. Then he had powered on up to the Top S. Before Barry had returned to the paddock his time had been announced. It had been much slower than the line through the Kennel had promised, 40.70 seconds.

When Barry had rolled down the hill and arrived back in the paddock, Laughton could see that he was terribly disappointed and angry with himself for spoiling his run with that one minor mistake which had cost him a fast time. His mother had done the thing Jessie always did best! She had fed him some of the ham sandwiches and given him some tea to drink. In fact, once Barry had started eating, all of them had joined in the picnic and soon with a bit of teasing banter Barry's good humour had been restored. It had however quickly become apparent that Barry intended to do better on his second run.

Now suddenly all the years in-between fell away and Barry is, in his mind, telling him how that last run was, through his eyes, that magical day.

'At last I reach the starting line for the second time. I am really keyed up ready now for this. It is now or never. Fane with his almost identical Frazer-Nash 'had it' on the hill earlier. His supercharger sheared on the Bottom S bend. I don't think I am going to overtake Raymond Mays' time. Effortlessly, Mays in the light grey ERA knocked a complete second off Fane's record for the Hill earlier. I feel my lips purse with concentration as adrenaline pumps through me. I am concentrating on the rev counter.

The timer puts the timing device board, the thing they call the 'hockey stick' because of its shape, under my front offside wheel. As soon as the wheel goes over it time will start to rush away and I must be fast on my way up the hill. I feel the wooden chock being thrust under the rear right wheel. I can let off the brakes now. I won't roll back. Jack Humphries seems to be hovering still, checking something at the rear and talking to Raymond Mays. The old fox has come to watch my start. I had better make it a good one.

'Right in your own time Barry,' the timer says to me. I feel the pulsating engine under my right foot. Let's at least get near them! I wind the revs up to four and a half thousand. I keep my eye on the rev-counter. The mounting roar is pure power and that power is mine. The engine roars in my ears. She is ready to be unleashed. I drop the clutch now ...... keep the throttle steady to get maximum traction ...... the twin rear wheels spin briefly but I balance them against the power. They grip the tarmac and with full traction I accelerate rapidly away from the start in first gear. I feel an instant thrill as I am pinned back into my seat by the sheer exhilarating power of the supercharged engine as it hurtles me forward. A few seconds and now here comes Kennel Bend. As the revs come up to screaming pitch I change up to second and attack the bend as it kinks the course to the left. No come on, go for it, don't lay off, keep your right foot down. Don't give the engine a moment's respite.

I hear the supercharger with its characteristic wailing like an energetic tearing of calico as I come out of the bend. Watch the revs. As they quickly reach six thousand I snatch third and prepare to take The Crossing. Exiting the bend with the engine on maximum torque I rocket up the narrow track towards the Bottom S minding the bumps so as not to unsettle the car as I approach my braking point. The revs are five-eight; faster than ever I remember. Out, out I steer her to the edge near the bottom of the steep green bank on my right. I brake and snatching second gear turn into the Bottom S taking a very tight apex. I must be neat here and exit the bend in the middle of the road. I take the bend clean and tidy this time. I feel I am on the edge of what is attainable. The back end is just out and I balance the over steer on the adverse camber feeding the power on progressively. The wheels are almost buckling as I feed the throttle on through the corner ...... and we're there ...... now foot to the floor in a quick spurt up to the Top S ...... come on set it up ...... as I turn in my nearside wheel just misses the drain grating on the apex ...... perfect ...... a touch here would have unsettled her. The tail is out now ...... I apply more power and push through the last right hander with my rear wheel almost touching the bank on the left ... and as the rev counter hits six I snatch third gear and head for the line extracting every ounce of power to cross the line at five-eight.

Whew! I am sweating with effort; I think that was quick! What was my time? What did the loudspeaker say? Couldn't hear a blasted thing with this helmet on but it felt fast. I pull into the semi-circle behind a Special and wait for the marshalls to send us back down the hill once the Class has completed their run.

Now where are my cigarettes? I am dying for a fag! I will have to wait until I am back in the Paddock before I know for sure. So frustrating!

I am definitely coming back next year now I am beginning to get the hang of it. By the time I am halfway through my smoke the Class have all finished. I hear the relay of whistles from the Marshalls on the Hill. I can imagine the red flags being put out to signal it is safe for us to return to the Paddock. Our Marshall now beckons us to start down and we roll down the hill back to the start one behind the other in a metallic snake. I turn into the newly finished return road just after Kennel bend and arrive back in the Paddock. As I park Jack Humphries is there waiting ready to tend to cooling the engine.

'So how did I do?' I shout as I approach. He is smiling and clearly excited. He then tells me that I have recorded my fastest run so far on the Hill; 40.30 seconds. 'Forty point three seconds,' I repeat with incredulity. I knew it had been fast but that is beginning to show what I really can achieve! Mother and you rush over to congratulate me. Remembering not to hold the steering wheel I clamber out of the car putting my feet on the seat; holding the side as I step out onto the ground. Mother hugs me. You are wreathed in smiles and pat me on the back. I could see you are really proud of what I had just achieved. Max is smiling and wanting to shake me by the hand. Raymond Mays comes over to join us in the Paddock and several passing well wishers slap my back, clearly pleased by my time.

'Barry that was a fine run,' Raymond Mays says, 'I shall have to watch that you don't overtake me on the hill!'

'Doubt if I will do that for a long time sir. You and your ERA perform just magnificently. But I will be trying even harder next year!"

Chapter 17

DINNER AND MAX!

Then afterwards there had been that dinner party. After Barry's success in the afternoon we all sipped champagne cocktails outside on the loggia at Palmers Hill waiting for the other guests to arrive. Max Hoffman came downstairs after changing and Laughton recalled thinking how dashing his boys had both looked in their dinner jackets. All the women had made an effort and there was elegance and beauty in abundance.

It had chilled quite quickly outside. Some of the girls had short sleeved dresses and their bare arms were showing goose pimples. At his suggestion they had moved into the drawing room and shut the loggia doors. A few minutes later Lavinia had arrived with her brother, Charles. Laughton had seen them earlier at Shelsley but only from a distance. Betty and her current boyfriend, Jimmy Gardener, had also been with them and had seen him and waved. He had not known she had intended coming to Shelsley. Having greeted Lavinia and Charles at the front door he had spoken briefly to Charles who had taken a nasty tumble from his horse a couple of days before. Then he led them into the drawing room.

He left them all for a moment to make sure all the bottles of red wine were open. By the time he returned the party was in full swing. He noticed that Mac had opened yet another bottle of champagne and was splashing it into the guests' glasses with gusto! They would all be drunk by the time dinner came if they went on drinking at this rate!

The family were of course all there but Jimmy Gardener, had returned to his home in Sussex as it was his mother's birthday on the Sunday. He had left them after their return from Shelsley in that blue Bugatti of his that Mac and Barry so admired. He recalled Jimmy telling him that its bodywork had been designed by Malcolm Campbell so that was probably why! Jimmy had bought it off Campbell that February when it had only done 800 miles. Jessie had asked their neighbours, the Wilkes at the last minute, so now they were all assembled there were ten for dinner.

They all went through to the dining room and consulting his crib he ushered Lavinia and Betty to the chairs to the right and left of him at the top of the table and Jessie to the foot. Next to Betty was Max, then Helen and Barry. Facing them were Mac next to Lavinia then Felix and Charles. It was good to see so many of his son's young friends around the table joining them. The first course was smoked salmon served on a bed of lettuce. As he went round serving that rather distinctive hock which Max had brought over from Germany as a gift from his father for them he heard the chatter.

The young were all talking about the day at Shelsley; the girls about who they had seen with whom; the boys about the high performance now reached with the superchargers such as had been fitted to the Frazer-Nash Barry had driven. The adults were happily joining in the various conversations and everyone was having fun. He had felt it was going to be a good evening.

The first course plates cleared, Elsie, the cook, brought in the joint on a large dish. With the carver he had sharpened earlier he began to carve what looked an excellent leg of lamb which Jessie had bought from Fred Mercer, the local butcher. Steaming bowls of locally grown vegetables were now on the mats in the middle of the table and as he passed the plates with their generous helpings of meat down the table he and Jessie encouraged them all to help themselves once served. He had difficulty in being heard above the laughter and loud chatter. Everyone seemed to be having a good time. The pudding was a new one which Jessie had spotted in some recipe book or other. Damson fool served in cut glass dishes that her grandparents had used when they were alive.

It was after eleven o'clock when they rose to let the ladies withdraw ostensibly to powder their noses and chatter amongst themselves. Jessie had never agreed with this protocol but reluctantly abided by it because she knew it was expected at that time. He remembered some pretty heated exchanges when they were younger after such occasions but this evening had gone so well that she withdrew without any of the caustic comment she was accustomed to make on such occasions!

There was port and brandy to be passed around the table. He offered La Paz cigars. Only Max and he lit up. The rest of the men had cigarettes from Mac who offered them from his own silver case, the one Jessie and he had given him a couple of Christmases ago. The cordial atmosphere was quieter now the women had left. It became more sombre when Charles asked Max his opinion on Hitler.

'Hitler.' Max had repeated in his guttural English drawing at length on his cigar, 'Hitler has done a lot of good for Germans.'

'In what way?' asked Felix.

'He has strengthened the economy and given us back our pride.'

'Hasn't that meant stealing from the Jews?' Charles came back at him.

'Pah ...... the Jews!' Max replied studying his cigar and avoiding eye contact, 'Hitler was right to remove their economic power. They were crippling our economy and who, I ask you, was benefiting .... of course the Jews!'

This conversation was moving fast into dangerous waters. He could see Felix was quietly seething. Felix had many staunch Jewish friends. He and Felix had only recently discussed what was happening in Germany in relation to Jewish interests. Felix had been vociferous in condemning the anti-Semitic tactics being promoted by the Nazis. If this conversation continued, down-to-earth Felix would not hold back and embarrassment could follow. He tried to change the subject to hunting as the Albrighton Hunt was meeting the following weekend and he genuinely wondered whether Charles would be riding after his recent fall. But soon after his intervention Felix had interrupted and deliberately turned the conversation back to Germany.

'Surely, the Jews were making money for Germany! What right did Hitler have to take away their wealth and input?'

'Every right ...... anyway it was a political decision! Hitler is a great leader. He has made us Germans proud to be German again.'

But then Mac had joined in.

'Winston Churchill ...... you know who I am talking about don't you ...... he is saying that Hitler is a warmonger; that he is building up your armed forces and air force in a way that makes the prospect of war with you almost inevitable.'

'Hitler doesn't want war with you. He is a great admirer of England. You are all Aryan like us. We need closer links so you can understand our thinking.' Max replied adopting a more conciliatory tone.

'Are you a fully paid up member of his Nazi Party, Max?' Mac was more direct this time.

'Yes I am ...... but what of it?'

'The Nazis are re-arming Germany ready for a war. That's what Mr Churchill is saying. You know that Barry and I fly as auxiliaries with the RAF. I have been reading the press reports from Germany. Your Luftwaffe air force is growing daily. It is huge and modern compared with ours; bombers and fighters in abundance. What are they for unless Hitler is planning a war?'

'We had our arms taken from us after the First World War. All we have done is to put together a force with which we can defend ourselves. No more, no less'

'I think that's hard to swallow. The new Messersmitt 109s are being produced by the hundred. You don't need them or your Junckers to defend yourselves. Anyway defend yourselves from whom?'

'We have our enemies! But this is ridiculous we don't need to talk like this as if we are enemies. You and I are friends Mac. We are all friends round this table, no?'

'We are at the moment Max.' Rejoined Mac, 'But what if our countries found themselves at war. We could find ourselves pitched against each other.'

Before Max could answer Barry interrupted jocularly.

'Yes Max I suppose you could be flying your Me 109 and I could be in some old Gladiator, dog fighting about the sky. What would you do then if you recognised me as the pilot you old renegade? Wave hello to me I suppose!?'

Max clearly resented the intervention and was still serious when he replied.

'No Barry I should do my duty!'

'Which would be to do what exactly?' asked Mac.

'I vould shoot you down!'

The remark had brought immediate silence. It had only been broken by some forced laughter after Mac had retorted, 'You'd never catch him!'

There had been one or two attempts to revive the conviviality of the evening but they had failed miserably. Max said he was tired and excusing himself went upstairs to bed. Felix had collected Helen and also left.

Chapter 18

THE RAF BECKONS

Like so many other young men of their acquaintance the boys from an early age had been enraptured by the idea of flight. Having learnt with Uncle Jack how to fly in their teens and then having had their father's Gypsy Moth to practice on they were both as proficient flying in the air as driving on the ground. In the early thirties he recalled how each of them could hardly wait to reach the age qualification to join the local auxiliary squadron, 605 Squadron, the 'Warwick Squadron'; part of the Auxiliary Air Force.

They had invited him on occasions to visit their base in Castle Bromwich in Birmingham where he had watched them flying Wapitis and later, Gloster Gladiators. Then just before War broke out they had come together to his study one day in August 1939. They had both been very excited; they had heard that 605's Gladiators were to be replaced by the new faster and better armed Hurricanes that everyone was talking about. They showed him their 'call up' papers. They were to report to their Squadron at Castle Bromwich on 24th August. Mac would join as a Flying Officer as he had much more experience flying than Barry who had often avoided summer training with the Squadron in favour of hill-climbing the Frazer-Nash. Barry would join as an Acting Pilot Officer. They knew their mother might be upset so the real purpose of their visit was to ask him to break the news to her.

When he had told Jessie she had not been so much upset as deeply concerned. He had not been able to share the depth of her concern but equally had found he could not share the boys' enthusiasm of wanting to have a 'go' at the Germans. It was clear now that the Nazis could not be stopped from all out war. Laughton had lost too many friends in the last conflict to be enthusiastic about any war. At least, he had thought to himself, in the air the boys would stand a better chance than serving in the infantry on the ground.

Within three days of Mac and Barry leaving Palmers Hill for Castle Bromwich they were in touch sharing the trunk call between them to say that their Squadron was being posted to RAF Tangmere.

The following Sunday was a bright and sunny day. Palmers Hill basked in the autumnal light but he and Jessie had been riveted to the wireless bulletins. They had sat in the drawing room at Palmers Hill listening to the BBC medium wave news on their Murphy Radio with its polished walnut cabinet. At ten o'clock the BBC had told them to stand-by for an announcement of national importance. Then the broadcasts of music and a talk about how to make the most of tinned foods had been interrupted by further announcements that the Prime Minister would speak to the Nation at a quarter past eleven.

Prompt at that time the radio crackled and then they had heard Neville Chamberlain's voice.

'I am speaking to you from the Cabinet Room at 10 Downing Street. This morning the British Ambassador in Berlin handed the German Government a final note stating that, unless we heard from them by eleven o'clock that they were prepared at once to withdraw their troops from Poland, a state of war would exist between us. I have to tell you now that no such undertaking has been received and that consequently this country is at war with Germany. Now may God bless you all. May He defend the right. It is the evil things that we shall be fighting against, brute force, bad faith, injustice, oppression and persecution and against them I am certain that the right will prevail.'

Whilst the normal programmes resumed he and Jessie had sat and talked.

'Don't worry dear it will probably all be over by Christmas' he had reassured.

'That is what they said last time Laughton and look what happened then! We had years of it! And I am worried about the boys.'

At the first opportunity he recalled turning their conversation to more distracting subjects like suggesting that they should build an Anderson shelter near the woodland behind the house. Jessie could not see much point in it and nor had he but it had been a good topic to alight on at that particular moment! Out in the country where there were no rail or munitions targets he could not see the likelihood of air raids at Palmers Hill even if the Germans could get as far as Worcestershire in their bombers. Of course, one was never built.

The following month Barry was posted to No 5 Flying Training School up at Shotwick near Chester where he stayed until the late April of the following year. From there it was quite easy for him to drive down to see them at Palmers Hill even on short passes. They trained him on Hawker Hart trainers. With its Kestrel engine the biplane was now well past its day but apparently they did not have enough Hurricanes to be able to train him on those. Training on Hurricanes would have wait until he was operational with his Squadron.

Barry had found the ground subjects distinctly boring. Flying on instruments he had quite enjoyed as it was flying related. Even with navigation he had just about coped but learning Morse Code had been a nightmare for him. Fortunately, the class room training had been secondary to flying which was really all Barry had wanted to do. As often as the weather would allow he had been airborne learning the nuances of attack and defensive evasion. The word had got around at the school that if the battle for the air over Britain was prolonged beyond a few months they might have to fight using the Harts with their two machine guns mounted on the sides. If that happened Barry had frequently said against the Me 109s they would stand as little chance as a snowball in Hell of not being blown out of the sky!

Laughton had been amused when at last Barry had gained his 'wings'. It had been on April Fools Day and when Barry had phoned Palmers Hill to tell them Jessie had thought he was teasing her! He had been fortunate to pass at all for Laughton recalled Barry eventually spilling the beans about his examination results at the end of his course. Basically, he had failed, only getting 75.4% in his ground subjects which were apparently below average. Barry had been very laid back about it and had laughed whilst telling him that he had only managed to save himself from rejection by his enthusiasm for flying. Fortunately for him that was regarded as excellent!

Anyway he had then been posted to re-join his Squadron who had been moved up to RAF Wick Caithness. 'Up' Laughton supposed was appropriate as UP he had just remembered was their aircraft identification code emblazoned on their fuselage! Intensive training on Hurricanes had followed immediately under the direction of 605's new CO, George Perry, who he had heard drove all of the pilots hard to get to battle readiness.

Flying as wing man to his flight leader Barry had recounted one lesson George had given him in the air. They had simulated an air battle in which they had attacked from the sun, diving from 20.000 feet. Sighting the 'enemy bombers' who were actually other planes from the Squadron they had learnt to deliver beam attacks with pretend three second bursts over the radio with pursuit after the 'bombers' had broken formation to put in further solid bursts of fire at close range to ensure that they were downed.

At 20,000 feet his hands particularly had been really cold. It was the cold that had led him to tell Laughton about the battle tactic lesson. Barry had actually collared Betty to ask whether she had any old laddered silk stockings she could let him have as no silk gloves were available. Otherwise, to keep the cold out he usually wore his fur lined Irvine jacket and just a pair of woollen gloves with leather gauntlets over the top! He said as they only had a couple of minutes to scramble he feared he might even have to fly in his pyjamas if he didn't have time to dress. Later he had told Laughton that at least twice during his forays over Dunkirk he had had to do just that with all his other kit on top!

Meanwhile Mac had also been training; first at No.1 Armament Training School at RAF Catfoss, near the East Coast where he had been given the opportunity to fly Spitfires. Laughton recalled how excited Mac had been when he had flown one for the first time and had told him how it was pretty hairy to land as you came in faster than in Glosters and you could not see forward once the aeroplane was over the runway! You had to turn into the runway at an angle so you could judge your position before straightening up for a three point landing and with a view only to your side, put her down.

Mac was then sent on to No1 Flying Practice Unit at Meir near Stoke on Trent in Staffordshire. Whilst there one of the boys' 48 hour passes had coincided so that both he and Barry had been back at Palmers Hill together sporting their 'wings' proudly. Betty had been so pleased to see them that she had made an iced sponge to celebrate. She and Jessie had spoilt them to bits and as a family he had taken them all out for a meal together at The Talbot in Belbroughton.

He recalled that the brother's talk had been dominated by the fact that our pilots were being killed all too easily by the enemy who seemed to have overwhelming numbers of planes and experienced pilots. Laughton had recalled how it had seemed to all of them that they were being overwhelmed by the enemy. 'Thank heavens' he recalled thinking, 'Churchill has taken charge'.

Chapter 19

DUNKIRK

He recalled how the British Expeditionary Force had been squeezed out of France by the Panzer divisions. Now somehow into his memories of that time came Barry's and Mac's own instant flashes of how with their Squadrons they had tried to protect the soldiers, so many of whom had later been rescued by that amazing armada of little boats.

Mac had been really pleased when the worry he and Barry had felt being pilots in the same Squadron had been ended by their separation. When he had discussed with his brother his fear that one of them would be killed if they both remained in 605 throughout the War, he was surprised to find that Barry had entertained similar thoughts. Mac was delegated to take the lead to change the situation. As a result both of them had found themselves in the Acting CO's office. Grant-Ferris had in his hand Mac's written application for a transfer.

'What's all this about you two?' he had asked quite curtly. Mac had explained and found that Grant-Ferris' attitude softened.

'Well we are all at risk at getting killed you know whichever squadron we are in!' he had concluded 'But if you both feel as strongly as this you will be a liability if you both stay with 605. I will try to arrange it, but no promises mind! I am saying I will try.'

There it had been left but soon afterwards Mac had received a posting to 609 Squadron; the West Riding Squadron which had the hunting cry 'Tally Ho' on their Squadron badge.

'I should be all right with them,' Mac had said to Barry when the news came through. Barry too had been pleased about the move. Mac eventually had transferred to 609 two days after the Squadron had moved to Northolt. It was the 20th May and a bright hot sunny day. It was only a day before Barry's Squadron was also ordered south to RAF Hawkinge in Kent. Almost immediately he had been up against Me 109s in action patrolling the Boulogne and Calais areas.

The jangle of the scramble bell and Barry was once again awake. He felt so very weary. Then they all did. This will be my fifth patrol today he thought. But then he remembered the poor sods waiting for the Navy to evacuate them from that beach. Thousand upon thousand of them. A whole Army. The memories of what he had already seen of the debacle instantly motivated him. Lets go again. Fast across the ground seconds later he was inside his plane once more. Jock Sutton, one of his ground crew, who claimed that he was Scots through and through but had never before stepped out of Aston in Birmingham, pulled away the chocks once the engine had started. He had been quick to taxi and take off with the rest of the squadron. The orders were to carry out a protective sweep over Dunkirk and Boulogne where enemy aircraft were annihilating the B.E.F.

Soon they were over the beaches. The visibility was clear; disastrously so for those waiting on the beach. The devastation was awful to behold in the extensive panorama they had from their vantage of several thousand feet. For mile upon mile behind the beachhead there was army debris of every type. Bedford lorries lay alongside anti-aircraft guns, howitzers and tanks abandoned, destroyed, burning. Black arid smoke reached even his nostrils as it rose to meet the clear blue May sky as if attempting to eclipse the sun which was pouring its afternoon heat onto the sands below.

Naval troop ships were trying to berth a little way out as a bridged phalanx of khaki clad men, some holding their rifles aloft over their heads to protect them from the brine, waded their way to where they were being picked up by lighters and ferried to the waiting vessels. They were totally vulnerable to air attack as indeed were the ships themselves and he could see a number of partly submerged hulls still smoking after their sinking in the fearsome air bombardment that had been rained down by the opposition. But worse still was the sight of those many men whose bodies littered the sands, lying where they had fallen when the German fighters had strafed the beaches earlier.

As they had dived towards the beaches men looked up and waved recognising their RAF roundels.

'Bandits at quarter to!' came his flight leader's voice over his headphones.

Looking to port he saw three Me. 109s intent on strafing the road that led directly to the beachhead and soldiers leaping for cover into the ditches that lined the sides as the planes left death and destruction in their wake. Abandoned vehicles littered the congested road and as the bullets raked them, occasionally one burst into flames just to add to the chaos that already existed down there.

Moving the stick to turn tightly he felt the G forces pin him back into his seat as the plane pulled round to port. Suddenly he was confronted by one of the Me. 109s tearing towards him at about 250 knots. Increasing his own throttle he feinted a dive and then brought the stick back so that for a split second he was under his adversary. His thumb marked out the enemy's belly with a thunderous barrage burst of his machine guns. The 109 slewed past him mortally wounded catching flame as it went and he felt his own plane judder as the waves of the sudden aerial explosion struck him from the side.

It had been over in an instant. Him or me! He later learnt that his leader had damaged one of the other 109s and the third had made off inland. He had not seen that part of the brief action. He made a last pass along the beach regaining his wing position with his leader as he did so.

Below them many of the soldiers were waving and gesticulating excitedly towards the fliers. They had seen his quarry go down in a ball of flame and that had sent their spirits soaring. Yet he felt no exhilaration at the kill; only that deep set cold numbness of battle weariness that sorts the living from the dead. It was going to be a tough week.

A couple more passes ensured that the 109s had indeed returned to their base. Only then did they all turn for home. The kill behind him, thoughts of a hot bath; a few jars and then perhaps some sex with that pretty blonde barmaid who fancied him at the Arms, filled his mind and stirred his loins. Their flight back over the south coast was uneventful and he landed without hazard. Only during their de-brief did he learn they had lost yet another pilot, George Middleton; that was the second in two days. Would it be his turn next?

Mac's first encounter with an enemy plane came at the very end of May when he flew in one of 609's many patrols over the French coast but he had not been as fortunate as Barry in catching one of the enemy fighters. Flying as part of 'B' Flight' on 31st May they had encountered a group of Messerschmitt Me.109s escorting Heinkels who were bombing the retreating Army below.

They had engaged them and as one of the 109s turned towards him Mac had seen red blobs coming at him from its nose and slowly the realisation had hit him that they were tracer bullets and that he was under fire! Some of the bullets streaked so close to his starboard wing that he had been able to see their trails of grey smoke as they spent themselves against the air and fortunately not against him!

The sudden terror he had felt had coursed the adrenalin. It had taken him a moment to suppress the fear that had unmanned him. Then in a more sudden and harder reaction on the controls than he had intended he had pulled his Spitfire round so tightly that the force drained the blood from his head and he was for a moment faced by a black curtain before he was able to regain control. His turn had in fact fortuitously brought him round behind another Me. 109. Mac had pursued him, brought him within range.

He had let off a burst of shells and thought a few had impacted with the enemy's port wing. He had seen the pilot in the cockpit of the 109 for a brief second, another human being, then the plane had twisted and turned away from him. Suddenly, another Spitfire was attacking the 109 head on and he was blown out of the sky. It had been one of the Spitfires from 'A' Flight. The pilot, he learnt later, had already downed one of the Heinkel He. 111s and now was able to claim a 109!

It had been a wake-up call. He had experienced that impulse to stay alive which whilst in one way was protective he had realised could also consume him with its attendant fear so that to be any use as a pilot it had to be overcome. He had re-joined his Flight in something of a panic wanting just to get home. The sight of the chalk cliffs of the English coast beneath him on their flight back had been particularly reassuring.

He had been in combat for the first time and it was only after the second mug of tea with copious spoonfuls of sugar at dispersal after landing that the intermittent trembling that had overtaken him on the flight back stopped. He had been under fire; seen a pilot downed; had heard of the Squadron's own losses that day, of two pilots against at least five enemy planes destroyed. He had come of age as a fighter pilot!

An even more important mission had been tasked to 609 on a night in early June about the 13th. He recalled it specifically as having been a couple of nights after he had been on a rare night out in London, relaxing with Novi and a couple of others from the Squadron. They had managed to get seats for the Windmill and more important, pass outs to go at a time when there was no leave being granted! The glamour of the beautiful scantily-clad high-kicking dancers and the vibrant music had lifted his spirits after the mayhem he had been constantly witnessing day after day during patrols over Dunkirk.

He had particularly missed seeing Nell at that time but they had kept in close touch by telephone when he could get through. Often that was difficult because of the vagaries of the telephone system. It could take up to five minutes to get through and then once the telephone was answered at Overton Hall another eternity before he would at last hear her soft voice. Nevertheless, his morale had been kept high by their spasmodic contact and occasional visits back to Palmers Hill on short pass outs.

He recalled the Sunday evening at Northolt. He had gone early to the kiosk to ring Nell only to find that the kiosk had been closed and that there was the usual notice on it which declared it was out of use! The Red Caps always put that notice on when there were particularly sensitive operations going on to doubly ensure that there was no leakage of information.

Annoyed he could not speak to Nell he had been going towards the Mess when he bumped into Mike Williams from A Flight.

'Hello Mac where the hell have you been? Flight is looking for you. All the rest are at Dispersal. There's a bit of a flap on. Not quite sure why yet but there is a rumour that there may be a night in Paris in it for those involved!'

So summoned he had gone immediately to find out what was happening. He found the other members of 'A' Flight at Dispersal. The rumour was that they were flying that night to escort some politician or other over to France. It was not long before they were briefed by Flight Lieutenant Howell who had been ordered to lead. He had told them the details. The nine of them were going to fly to Warmwell the next day to rendezvous on the Tuesday with a twin-engine de Havilland Flamingo which would be coming from Hendon. They would then escort the plane to a small airfield in the vicinity of Briare, not far from Orleans. They would have to get such sleep as they could at the airfield as they would be returning at dawn the following day. Their charge was not disclosed at that time but there was a rumour that it might be Winston himself, and so it turned out!

By Tuesday early evening they were all at Warmwell close to the coast of Dorset ready to take off. Warmwell was to play a more important part for 609 a month or so later. They were by their planes as the Flamingo from Hendon was brought in making a perfect landing into the wind on the grass runway. As soon as it had come into view they had gone to their planes. A bowser had gone to the Flamingo when it had come to a halt. No one alighted but it had been refuelled at speed by members of the ground crew. Then taking orders from their leader they all took off into the wind.

They had taken a circuitous route out to the west of France to avoid the risk of enemy aircraft. The precaution was successful save on the return flight, for as they had passed close to a burning Le Havre to their right they had been forced to reduce their height and had spotted a couple of German aircraft well below them focussed on strafing some fishing boats.

Notwithstanding just that one scary moment Mac had recalled how he had been personally totally on edge throughout the trip over to France and during the return journey the following dawn. He had bunked down with the other pilots in a train near to where the politicians were meeting at a Chateau, but hardly slept. They did not make Paris but fortunately there was a bistro nearby which served their needs, at least so far as wine was concerned! Fortunately neither the flight there in the twilight nor the flight back in the pinkie grey of the dawn attracted any attack from enemy aircraft. The major problems had involved getting sufficient fuel to get them all back and having to crank each other's engines because of a lack of battery power!

After they had eventually flown back and landed thinking only of showers and breakfast, Winston had insisted on coming to where they were drinking tea and writing up their logs. He had wanted to thank the men who had guarded him safely to France and back. It was a typical Churchillian gesture. He had put them all quickly at ease and spoken briefly in general terms of the importance of his mission to France. It had turned out later that he had been meeting the French Prime Minister, Paul Reynaud, Marshal Petain and others. Then he was gone and Mac had not seen him again. It was a real feather in the Squadron's cap that they had been chosen. The inspiration that he left behind had been dynamic and long lasting. Days later France had finally sought an armistice with Hitler and so the Battle for France had ended.

Chapter 20

A TRAGIC ACCIDENT

605 had been so badly mauled and had lost so many pilots whilst patrolling over Dunkirk that we were pulled back to re-group at RAF Drem near Edinburgh. There on Sunday 23rd June two planes were lined up on the Parade Ground.

It had been the Padre's idea for morning service. The one was a Spitfire and the other a Hurricane. Both had been polished up and looked immaculate. The Hurricane was the one which I usually flew. The Squadron assembled and the Padre took the morning outdoor service. A strong easterly wind from the Urals that day made the air feel chilly even though it was high summer. The entire Squadron sang and prayed and the Padre blessed the planes and sprinkled holy water over them.

I really paid little attention to it all. Unlike Mac, although subjected to the same Christian upbringing I did not have much of a faith. If any remained from school days it had been brutally knocked out of me by recent events. After the service, in the bar I drank my usual pint of Flowers ale. A few of the other pilots ribbed me telling me that I must now be safe from harm as God had blessed my plane! The next morning the polished Spitfire overshot the runway and pitched nose up in the hedge at the far end. So much for blessings! Anyway I was not required until the evening and that was only on exercises experimenting with those new twilight landing lights.

Good old Batchy, our glorious CO, Wing Commander Richard Atcherley! A great practical joker but what an exceptional pilot and his charisma, well that was something else besides! He was clearly going places if he survived. He had come up with this bright idea that would get our bombers in safe from marauders at night. Some of the enemy fighters had been picking off returning bombers just as they were coming in to land and most vulnerable.

Batchy had conceived the idea of forming a flight path with flares at different intervals so you knew exactly what height you were flying at and could come in faster and land safely, more quickly. The flare path could only be seen by aircraft coming in on approach to the strip below 500' so it told you what you could not otherwise see! 605 of course got the job of testing out all the variations of the idea. It was always, therefore close to twilight when you went up. And it was pretty boring stuff being called in sequentially to land and then take off again and do it all over again! Several times a night!

Come the 24th June we had been doing it on and off since we had come back from Dunkirk to get our wind back. By that Monday all the damage to the planes had been repaired. We all wanted to see some more action. I suppose we wanted revenge for losing so many mates during the Dunkirk debacle which had really knocked us about and was the reason we were stuck up at Drem.

I had been in touch – if you can call a three minute trunk call 'being in touch' – with Mac. 609 were enjoying warm sunny days down at Northolt. Reading between the lines of what he told me on the telephone – he had to be careful about what he said – they were expecting the Luftwaffe to launch a big air bombing offensive to soften up the south of England and follow it up with invasion. Anyway that was also the word that was going around. 'Invasion!' The very thought of it turned me cold as I thought of Mum, Dad and Betty at Palmers Hill. And I am stuck up here at Drem. Where is the use in that?

These melancholic thoughts are interrupted by us being called to the briefing by the CO in the main building. It takes us much longer than I expect to get over there with Harry Oldfield and Walter Churchill. This drome is so bloody large it takes for ever to get around. And it's much colder up here in the evenings. I wish I had put my flying jacket on. We arrive late and as we go in and take our seats we get one of Batchy's looks. He had just started; so for our benefit he summarises what he has already covered with thinly veiled sarcasm in our direction. But it's all the same as the other nights. Why doesn't he just tell us to go out and do the same thing again! We are all highly experienced pilots now and he is treating us like kids. Well that's how I feel. I vaguely listen whilst he drones through the slight changes he has made to the lights and then the various usual warnings. 'Yeah, Yeah we've got all that Batchy,' I mouth but do not dare say out loud. I respect him too much. Soon we are all outside again.

'Spoke to Mac last night. Took twenty minutes to get through. He hinted that they are making a big build up across the Channel.'

'Yes I know.' Harry replies, 'What the hell are we doing 'twilight landings' for up here? They need us down south surely?'

'My thoughts exactly! But there is nothing we can do about it is there? We shall just have to continue doing this night after night.'

'Well I suppose we could have a bit of flying practice as well.'

'What do you mean 'flying practice'?'

'Well I was doing a few stall turns and one or two diversionary manoeuvres whilst waiting my turn to be called in last time. How about you? Come on it's not like you Barry not to be doing something a bit adventurous. Are you getting a bit staid in your old age?' Harry laughed.

'Oh I have been pretty good lately. Batchy grounded me if you remember when last time he heard I had done a loop. But a few stall turns .... perhaps I could get away with that and it certainly would liven things up a bit going into a dive or two!'

As we speak we each take a cigarette from the packet Harry is holding out to me. Harry then strikes a match and cupping his hands, lights mine first then his own. In the pause thus formed others join us and the banter and chat move on to other topics. Soon it is time for us all to go to Dispersal. Once in my plane the gloom that I had felt earlier evaporates. This is where I always love to be and where I feel most at home these days. The Merlin starts first time. The ground crew give me the 'thumbs up' as they pull the chocks away. The crackle over my radio breaks into commands from the Control Tower and I respond in similar form.

I join my Flight and taxi out to the end of the runway staying close to my flight leader. We three turn almost together as one and once we have clearance from the Tower we all open our throttles and speed into the wind. I always find this moment exhilarating as the plane's speed effortlessly picks up and pins me back into my seat. I feel the tail lift and now I can see the runway ahead running before me. Then at just over 60 knots I ease the stick back gently and the plane rises like a bird into the sky. I retract the undercarriage and climb steadily with the others to 8000'. Together we all fly westwards on our usual flight path and we are soon over the Lammermuir Hills whose forested slopes interspersed with their green bracken and gorse lands lie below. Then we turn and await our orders to come in line astern and land.

I am waiting again, waiting! Control takes the other two flights in first and then at last it is our turn. The sun has dipped and will set soon. The whole sky is lit up with blue tinged with scarlet rays around the dipping sun and is ever changing now to a glow where there will be twilight very soon.

'Blue Three come in now.'

My wandering thoughts quickly focus again on the job in hand and I move the stick forward and pull in about half a mile behind Blue Two. The lights below at the moment are still a joke. They have been lit too early tonight. We do not need them yet. Still this is the first practice run so there it is. Have to do it. Undercarriage down. Within a few minutes I land only to be ordered to take off again immediately, so back into the air I go!. Two more runs to make. Blue leader has not come up again. His engine is playing up. I hear over the radio something about a malfunctioning oil pipe. Blue Two is just above me over to starboard. Again we fly the circuit and the frustration builds waiting for the order to land.

Right, now I land and take off again. One more to do and then a few beers in the Mess before turning in. Early start tomorrow. Its well after 9 o'clock now and the sun is just a memory for another day. The sky has that greyness of twilight that is the harbinger of night. At the horizon it merges the land into the sky. I have lost sight of Blue Two but he is still talking to me over the radio so he is not far away. The visibility will make those lights useful now. The wait this time is interminable. Control says they are actually relighting some of the flares! I wish they would get on with it.

Another call from Control. Its going to be another ten minutes before we can be called down. Ten bloody minutes! What are they playing at! My fuel gauge is still well above half so that's all right. A little amusement I think! Where are we? There is Innerwick set in the vale where the Lammermuir Hills rise beyond casting their shadow now over the village. 5500' so plenty of room. Lets try a few stall turns. Here we go, throttle back, lift the nose; listen to the engine. The engine quietens and as it finally dies I push the stick to port and start to dive. The engine does not re-start …… it will in a moment just touch the rudder to starboard and stop this spin. What the blazes was that? It looks like I am losing a gun panel from the port wing. Who didn't fasten it properly?

I can cope I am sure I can. Bit more rudder …… why isn't the f**king engine starting …… I am down now to 3000' already! Come on start damn you, start! Must have heard me, it splutters …… at last it fires. I punch the throttle to give maximum power. The spinning is less now but this doesn't feel right. I am not getting full power. There is black exhaust smoke coming out of the side of the engine cowling. What the hell is wrong? I have the stick right back now and the plane is just not pulling out of this dive. Can I bale out? No. Help I think it's too late for that. Oh thank God full power is back! I may still get out of this. Yes the nose is coming up but I am into the dusk. Christ this is a hill ……… No!

Chapter 21

ENQUIRY – PART ONE

They had last seen Barry at the beginning of June. He had hardly arrived at Palmers Hill on his 48 hour pass when it was time for him to turn around and head back to Drem. They had had little time to discuss anything serious. Laughton did recall though that he had been somewhat horrified to see how badly Barry had aged since they had seen him two months earlier just after he had obtained his 'wings'. It was hard to believe that he was still in his early twenties.

Early on the morning of Tuesday 25th June they had received that telegram. He recalled hearing whistling as the young Post Office lad had cycled up the drive on his red bicycle to deliver it. Laughton often had telegrams delivered at home and he knew from the whistling who it would be when he answered the door. He had been right. It was Gerald Ingram whose parents lived in the village.

He had handed Laughton the telegram and had asked him to sign for it making some innocent remark about the weather. Laughton had signed the docket, taken the telegram from Gerald's outstretched hand, said 'goodbye and returned into the house and smiled as he had heard Gerald's whistling grow fainter as the youth sped down the drive.

In the hallway he had put his glasses back on and seen it was an official telegram. He opened it and read its two terse sentences set out in capitals in a moment:

'REGRET TO INFORM YOU THAT YOUR SON NO 90504
PO B L GOODWIN KILLED IN FLYING ACCIDENT WHILST
ON ACTIVE SERVICE STOP DESIRE TO EXPRESS DEEPEST
SYMPATHY STOP LETTER TO FOLLOW – CO NO 605
SQUADRON'.

He had been so completely stunned that he had had to reach out and draw up a chair to sit down. It had been there that Jessie had found him a minute or so later with his head in his hands.

'Whatever's the matter, Laughton? Are you all right?' As he raised his head and looked towards her she had seen the telegram in his hand. Now looking frightened she had asked, 'Bad news?'

He had not been able to reply save to say 'The worst my love!' She had taken the telegram from him and read it herself as he stood up, put his hand on her arm and waited for her reaction.

'Oh no …… no no no … it can't be right! I can't bear it, not my Barry!' She had almost screamed as tears started to course down her cheeks and she came to him for the security of his embrace. He had just been able to catch her to support her as the intense shock hit her and she almost collapsed within his arms. They had then cried together and time had stood still.

Somehow they had managed to tell Betty who had immediately run up to her room in floods of tears. Laughton had followed her to talk to her but he had found her bedroom door locked and all he could hear were her sobs as the anguish of the moment poured out of her.

They later learnt that a Court of Enquiry into what had happened was set to take place at RAF Drem on Thursday 4th July. Laughton had been asked to attend the day before to identify Barry's body. He had asked to be allowed to attend the enquiry and the man he had spoken to on the telephone had said that would be in order. So on the Wednesday he had caught the fast express train from New Street Station in Birmingham to Edinburgh at 10am expecting to arrive at about 4pm.

Unfortunately, due it was said to troop movements in the north of England and some bomb damage to one of the lines the journey took much longer and he did not arrive until just before 6pm. There had been no restaurant car on the train. Even if there had been one he would not have been able to get much in the way of wholesome food these wartime days. On arrival in Edinburgh he had taken a taxi for the journey to Drem. All in all it had been a long wearisome journey and when he arrived at The Cottage Hospital he was tired and hungry. By then it was nearly seven in the evening.

An RAF officer, it turned out to be the one he had spoken to on the telephone, was waiting for him in the small reception hall and took him into the hospital's mortuary in the basement. A mortuary attendant wearing a badly stained white coat had led them to a room where there were several tables on which were obviously bodies beneath white sheets. There had been a cold chill in that room which had magnified the terrible apprehension that beset him as he now approached the particular table the attendant had led him to.

On a nod from the officer whose name he now remembered as Radford the attendant pulled back the sheet. There against the cold marble slab was Barry's neat blond hair matted with blood at the side of his head. His eyes were closed and although he had clearly suffered a terrible injury he looked as peaceful as if he was just asleep.

Laughton turned away his eyes brimming with tears. 'Yes' he heard his voice whisper a hoarse response to the officer's question 'is that your son Barry Laughton Goodwin sir?'

He turned back to the table thinking that he ought in some way to say 'farewell' to his dear boy. But the white sheet was firmly back in place and he somehow could not bring himself to ask for it to be removed again. As the thoughts had flashed through his mind Radford had taken his arm and he had staggered as he had been led from the room tears streaming down his face; his vision completely impaired.

'I'm so sorry' he had uttered by way of apology as he sought the protective veil of his handkerchief.

'No need for that sir' said Radford himself visibly swallowing apparently also finding this experience personally difficult.

'Where are you staying tonight sir?' he had asked deflecting the conversation and allowing Laughton gratefully to recover some of his normal equilibrium.

'I don't know. I haven't booked anywhere. I thought that I would be able to find a local pub or bed and breakfast place. Do you know of any where I could stay at this time of night?'

'Certainly sir, in fact I made a provisional booking for you at the Manse just opposite the gates to the station in case you had nowhere to stay. I hope you don't mind. Mrs Gaskell often puts people up there and does a good dinner in for the price. You will be all right with her.'

Laughton breathed a sigh of pure relief. He was already dreading finding a place to stay and this kind young chap who could not have been much older than Barry had sorted it out for him.

'Thank you, thank you very much. So kind,' and the sentiment of kindness brought back the tears.

His taxi had passed the station's gates earlier as he had arrived in Drem. One could not miss it with the guards in uniform outside sentry boxes and the white barrier bar down against the traffic. At each side of the wide entrance were big signs saying 'RAF Drem'. He would collect his overnight bag which he had left in the reception hall and get another taxi to the Manse. The taxi driver was almost certain to know it.

As these thoughts were going through his head he was aware that Radford was looking at his watch and had started to excuse himself saying that he had to meet the senior officer, Group Captain Torrance, who would be conducting the Enquiry. Laughton had asked him where he could get a taxi. Radford had immediately offered a lift with himself to the Manse on his way back to the station and Laughton had gratefully accepted.

Chapter 22

ENQUIRY – PART TWO

It seemed that Group Captain Torrance had travelled to the station at Drem the same day as Laughton. No doubt before dinner the previous day he had been briefed by Radford after Laughton had been dropped off at the Manse. The Court of Enquiry had been convened under the Board of Enquiry Rules of the time and Radford had been assigned the duty of organising the Enquiry, calling the evidence and recording the Enquiry's findings.

Amongst the documents Radford would have had with him at the time of the briefing would have been the RAF Casualty Card which recorded that the accident had occurred at 2100 hours on 24th June. The cause of the accident written on the card that very night, the night of the crash, was that the pilot had blacked out or hit his head against the cockpit side whilst he was doing unauthorised stall turns at 5000' and then the plane had gone into a spin dive from which it had never recovered. But it had also said on the card that the explanation was surmise. Laughton did not see that explanation until after the Enquiry was long since over and he had managed to get a copy of the RAF Casualty Card.

When Squadron Leader Torrance had entered the room at 1000 hours that Thursday morning at the beginning of July 1940 the personnel already there rose and stood to attention. Laughton recalled that Torrance had appeared to like that in the way he had almost preened himself. It made some people feel good watching people being subservient and to Laughton this was one such person. He had watched as Torrance's presence was acknowledged by those in uniform and then removing his service cap he had sat and motioned the others to regain their seats. He had looked towards where Laughton was sitting in the area behind those in uniform and then turned away almost as if in contempt that a relative might be present.

Meanwhile Flight Lieutenant Radford was on his feet introducing the Enquiry. Torrance was paying very little attention. It was obvious Radford was not used to conducting an enquiry but had probably been pressed into it by his CO. At first, he was hesitant and his introduction as to what had happened was heavy on detail but light on the real reason for the crash. Then he called his witnesses to the accident and its aftermath to give their evidence.

The first witness called was the doctor who presented a brief report which gave the cause of death as a fractured skull and multiple injuries including fractures of both legs and pelvis. It appeared that the cervical vertebrae had been partly forced upwards into the skull. Radford was gaining in confidence now. It seemed that Torrance felt he was asking unnecessary questions for he had stopped him. Laughton remembered the questions being asked just before Radford was interrupted.

'......and doctor was death instantaneous?'

'It would have been yes.'

'Consistent with the plane he was piloting hitting the ground?'

'Yes'

'Were there any burn marks on the body you examined?'

'No.'

'None?'

'That is correct.'

It was at that point that Torrance intervened.

'Yes, thank you doctor we need not detain you any longer.'

'......but I was going to ask ......' Radford had interjected.

'I think we have all the evidence we require from the doctor. I am sure he is needed elsewhere. Call your next witness.' There was an emphasis on the word 'next' which Radford had picked up on and thus rebuked, only with a show of slight reluctance did he call Alistair Whitehead to the table being used for the witnesses to sit at. The witness was just a boy. Torrance was there again.

'Should I be hearing from this witness Mr Radford?'

'Sir, he is the only person who saw the plane come down and is able to give clear evidence about it.'

'How old is he?'

'Nearly twelve,' the witness answered loudly as if the question was directed at him.

'Oh very well but he need not be sworn!'

Radford started his examination acquiring a few personal details as to his name, address where he went to school and the like. It turned out that the boy and his younger brother Duncan who was only seven originated from London. Their father had died during the fighting in France. The boys and their mother had taken refuge with her sister who lived in Innerwick village when their own house in the Mile End Road had been destroyed by a bomb landing on a munitions factory nearby. The boy identified his mother at the back of the room who had brought him that morning. From her oral acknowledgement Laughton put her down as being Scottish.

'Now tell us in your own words what happened?'

'Well me and Duncan, that's me brother we were playing up in the wood like near Innerwick like and then we got separated and that's when I heard the noise like.'

'What noise Alistair?'

'It sounded like a roaring engine and then it went quiet like. I looked up and I saw this plane.

'Do you know what sort of plane it was?'

'Oh yes, it were a Hurricane, one of them new planes.'

'Where was the plane?'

'In the sky silly,' Alistair's mother looked disapprovingly at her eldest son. Torrance stopped writing his note and said.

'Now young man, just behave. You don't speak to Flight Lieutenant Radford like that!'

The witness' head went down 'Sorry!' he had said in a low voice.

'Where was the plane in the sky?' The question came again.

'High up over me head. It were spinning round and round and then it stopped spinning and I heard the engine again like. The plane was much lower by then and I thought it were going to hit the ground.'

'What happened then?'

'Well I was looking at it all the time now and it started as if it were flattening out but then it went into the side of the hill like. I thought it were going to hit me so I hid behind a tree like. I looked out and saw its wingtip hit a high oak tree and then it went out of my sight.'

'Yes?'

'There were a bloody big bang when it hit the hill and I were frightened but I ran out and called to Duncan.'

'Did you see what happened to the plane when its wing hit the tree?'

'Yes, well it came off like.'

'Which wing was it?'

'I think it were the one on the left.'

'Are you sure about that?'

'Yeah pretty sure. Them pilots call it port don't they?'

Radford had ignored the question.

'What did you do then?'

'Well I ran down the hill. The plane was in one of the rides like all bust up and smoking. I thought it were going to catch on fire. There were bits of the plane all over everywhere.'

'Could you see the pilot?'

'Oh yes he were still in the cockpit like.'

'So what did you do?'

'Well I called to Duncan to help me and he came like and then we went to the plane. The plane were tipped over on its side and the top were open a bit so we managed to open it a bit more and we hauled this pilot out like.'

'Did you have to undo any straps to get him out?'

'No, but we had to get his harness undone.'

'And how did you manage that?'

'Me uncle works on the station here and one day he sat me in a cockpit like and did up the pilot's harness. It were great but I remembered that it did up funny and you had to hit it with your fist to undo it, so that's what I did like.'

'What exactly did you do?'

'Can I have a drink?' the witness looked round as if hoping his mother would produce a drink for him. A glass of water was produced and he took a sip. It was clearly not what he had been hoping for. He coughed and then continued.

'I belted this ring like and the harness came undone. Then we hauled him out like and pulled him away from the plane in case it caught fire. That's what me uncle told me happens when planes crash.'

'Did you notice anything about the pilot as you got him out?'

'He weren't saying nothing. He had blonde hair. I see'd he had blood on the side of his head. Duncan told me later that he thought he were dead but I didn't know that. His legs were all funny though.'

'What do you mean by that?'

'Sticking out like.'

'And then what happened?'

'Well suddenly there was another big bang and the plane like exploded and we felt the heat as we pulled him further away like.'

'Anything else after that?'

'Duncan put his jacket over him to keep him warm. He felt coldish to me. Then we could see grown-ups running up the hill from the village to where we were like. They took us away down home to me mam' and the witness pointed to his mother still sitting at the back.

Duncan was not called to give evidence as he was regarded by everyone as too young. It seemed anyway from what was said that he hadn't seen as much as his brother. He had been amongst the trees deeper in the wood than his brother when the plane had come down. Laughton had guessed that his view would have been obscured by foliage.

Radford then called the engineer who had examined the plane after it had been recovered to Drem following the accident. His name was David Fitzpatrick. The introductory questions elicited how he had been investigating flying accidents for over a decade. He himself, had trained in the RAF and worked his way through the ranks, in the process doing a degree in engineering in his own time. He was now a Squadron Leader based at RAF Lechars. He had examined the wreckage of the Hurricane L2115 the previous week after the Accident Team had brought it in from the site five miles south of Dunbar where it had crashed. It seemed that painstakingly he had put as much of it back together as he could during his examination to try and ascertain the cause of the crash. Radford moved on ......

'What type of engine was the plane fitted with?'

Fitzpatrick looked at Group Captain Torrance and made his replies to him.

'Merlin Type three sir.'

'Did you examine the engine?'

'Yes I did sir.'

'Did you find anything that might have contributed to the crash?'

'No sir, I didn't.'

'Nothing at all?'

'Well there was some oil marking which had burnt on the housing from a burst oil pipe but I was satisfied that had occurred when the plane crashed and then caught fire. I was able to take the engine apart despite some fire damage and when I examined the inner workings there was nothing that made me think that there had been a malfunction which had contributed to the crash.'

'If the pilot had been doing stall turns what effect would that have had on the engine's performance?'

'Well, as he reached the stall sir the engine would have stalled, but as soon as the nose went down the engine would have started again. I understood that he was at 5000' so he had plenty of time to then come out of any dive but there was one matter ......'

'The upper port wing gun panel?' Radford interjected.

'Yes sir, it's in my report. I found that the upper port wing gun panel had come off prior to the impact with the ground.'

'If the panel had come adrift at 5000 feet what effect would that have had on the controls?'

'Well sir, from my own flying experience, I would say it would have acted as a brake for a millisecond before becoming fully separated from the wing putting the plane into a spin. But this plane was being flown by an experienced pilot. He had flown something like forty-five hours in Hurricanes and would have corrected such a spin at least by the second turn. It would have been second nature to do so. He wouldn't even have had to think about it.

'How would he have corrected the spin?'

'He would have put on full left rudder, full right aileron and dipped the nose to get the speed up as quickly as he could. Having corrected the spin he would have pulled the stick back and with the height he still would have had the plane should have come out of the dive.'

'But this Hurricane ploughed straight into the ground?'

'Well not exactly sir, not straight into the ground. I recall only one plane in my experience of accidents actually having dived straight into the ground. It left a crater twelve feet deep. That plane was completely destroyed by the impact. This plane L2115 on the other hand had its port wing torn off but that was caused by a collision with a tree during its descent. The way in which the damage markings were distributed on this plane's fuselage suggest to me that it had or was flattening out of the dive we have heard about.'

'Have you examined the Maintenance 700 book as part of your investigation?'

'I asked for it to be produced sir, but I was told it has been lost.'

'Lost?'

'Yes sir.'

'So you have not been able to check on what servicing had been done to the plane recently?'

'No, well not from the book sir. I was able to ask the ground crew what they recalled of the work done on this particular aircraft.'

'What did you glean from those enquiries?'

'I was most interested at first, in who had last replaced the upper wing gun panel. Each is held by four quarter turn fasteners that you push in and twist to lock. They are then flush with the wing. I was told that the plane had been polished up for a Church Parade the day before the crash – that would have been Sunday 23rd – but no one admitted to having had the gun panel off at that time.'

'Was the plane armed at the time you examined it?'

'No sir, it was not. It did not need to be armed. It was taking part in twilight landings as part of experimental work being carried out at Drem. I know nothing more about that sir, as the information is classified. I do understand though that the pilot had already made two landings and was waiting to be called in for his third. It would have been his last for the evening.'

'Do we know when that panel was last put back?'

'No sir, without the 700 or a specific recollection we cannot know.'

At this point Torrance intervened.

'It doesn't matter anyway does it; you have said that the plane would still have been responsive to the controls if the pilot had done what he should have done. Isn't that correct? That is what I have noted. I have read your report. Basically, what you are saying is that there was nothing wrong with the aircraft?'

'Yes sir that is what I have reported.'

'Mr Radford do move on ......'

The Flight Lieutenant looked a bit put out but was sensible enough not to be irritated by the intervention. However, he quickly concluded his examination of the witness who then left.

The next witness was Pilot Officer Harry Oldfield who recounted the conversation he had had with Barry Goodwin just after the briefing on the night of the accident. He had not been in the air himself at the time of the accident so was not able to give an eye witness account.

'Your orders were to practise twilight landings. Is that correct?'

This question came from Torrance.

'Yes sir.'

'But you and Goodwin thought you would do a few aerobatics whilst waiting to go in?'

'I would not call a few stall turns 'aerobatics', sir.'

'What would you call them then?'

The witness paused, 'The sort of evasive flying which we would use in combat.'

'Nonsense, and even were that true, you were both disobeying your clear orders, weren't you?' Torrance looked hard at Oldfield and almost dared him to answer a negative.

This time the answer was quietly delivered almost in a whisper,

'Yes sir, you are right and I blame myself ...... I will always blame myself for what I said that evening.'

Torrance sat back in his chair with what appeared to Laughton at the time to be almost an air of triumph.

The Commanding Officer of 605 Squadron, Squadron Leader Walter Churchill was then called. He presented as a tall, handsome figure who had been quietly watching from the side during the proceedings. He could not have been very old. Laughton took him as being in his late twenties. Already there was grey at his temples. Again Laughton was struck by how this War was ageing this generation so very fast. Churchill now took the oath and sat waiting patiently whilst Radford collected up some notes he obviously wanted to refer to. After establishing background information about how Barry came to be part of the Squadron Radford's questions moved to more recent events.

'The Squadron was withdrawn from RAF Hawkinge then on 28th May?'

'Yes it was. We had taken a pasting the previous week over Dunkirk. We had lost a number of pilots and planes. The Squadron was exhausted and the planes so badly shot up we were withdrawn to Drem to allow us to regroup.'

'And Pilot Officer Goodwin?'

'He had been through it all with us. His contribution to both the sorties and to the morale of the Squadron was immeasurable. He ....'

Torrance came in at that point.

'...... disobeyed orders you had given him?'

'No not when we had been in battle. I often flew sorties with him. He was an outstanding natural pilot.'

'He failed his technical papers at Training School?' Torrance rejoined.

'Yes I know, but pilots of his quality aren't made by passing exams. Anyone seeing him in the air would have realised as I did, that this pilot was one who had a natural ability for flying in the way he handled his plane.'

'According to Oldfield you had grounded him once before for looping the loop. Had he been disobeying orders on that occasion?'

'In the strict sense 'yes' but I want you to understand that I only acted on that occasion because it had been reported to me and discipline demanded action by me. I think I actually grounded him for just a day!'

'That was when you were at RAF Hawkinge?'

'No it was after we had come to Drem. But a certain latitude needs to be allowed in dealing with such matters. The pilots are recovering the confidence they lost over France. The experiments we have been conducting with this new landing system are boring to the extreme. I know that. Many of the pilots are kept hanging around for long periods of time before being brought in whilst the lights are reconfigured or changed. These are young men full of 'go' and I am not in the least surprised to hear that one or two have let off steam by doing a few unauthorised manoeuvres whilst they waited.'

'It sounds to me that you have been slack with discipline?'

This remark coming from someone not in the front line clearly annoyed Churchill who replied angrily and instantly.

'Not at all. I am commanding an operational squadron whose combat readiness needs to be restored. Please don't tell me how to run my Squadron and when to apply the brakes. I think I know my chaps better than you and every one of them may have to give their life to ensure that our values survive. And I know each of them would willingly make that sacrifice.'

Torrance was silenced for a moment taken aback by Churchill's outburst. The silence permeated the whole proceedings and Laughton thought that you could have heard the proverbial pin drop! Then Torrance continued only slightly less aggressively.

'But on this occasion Pilot Officer Goodwin was doing something that he was not supposed to be doing ...... in disobedience to your orders... yes?'

'Strictly speaking yes, but you have heard what I have to say on the topic.'

Radford regained his witness.

'You effectively would have turned a blind eye to what happened that night if there had not been a crash. Is that what you are telling us?'

'I must be completely honest with you. Yes, in the circumstances existing at that time unless I had received an official report and been forced to take some action.'

'So how would you categorise Pilot Officer Goodwin as a pilot?'

'In a word he was outstanding. I am still very surprised from what I have heard that he was not able to correct his plane and avoid the crash. I don't think we shall ever know what really caused this accident.'

'Is there anything you would wish to add?'

'Only that I am aware that his father is here today and on behalf of all of the Squadron I would like him to know how much his son was valued as a member of the Squadron. Our thoughts are with him and his family at this time.'

'Thank you for that.'

A message had been brought into the room by a young woman and it had been passed to Radford.

'May I have a moment please, sir.'

'Yes but make it quick' retorted Torrance impatiently as he was glancing downwards at some papers he had made notes on. Radford read the message and then said.

'I have just this moment received a message from the engineer who gave evidence earlier. He would like to be recalled. There is a matter relating to his evidence which he would like to alter.'

Torrance was clearly irritated by the request coming at the end of the evidence and just before he was about to deliver his judgement about the accident.

'I think we have heard all the evidence that is important Mr Radford. What is the nature of the topic that Fitzpatrick wishes to canvas?'

'I am afraid the message does not tell me sir but I believe it is something to do with the port wing.'

'I have heard all about the port wing. The gun panel came off. Nothing to do with why this plane crashed.'

'I would ask you to hear this evidence just in case it throws new light on the issue.'

'No Mr Radford it is quite clear to me why this plane crashed and I will not be further assisted by some detail about a gun panel coming adrift.'

'For the sake of completeness sir, I do ask you to reconsider ………'

Torrance interrupted him.

'I have made my ruling clear Mr Radford and expect you to accept it!'

Radford clearly did not accept it but as Laughton could see there was no point in him arguing with this bigot any further. Radford sat down. Laughton had wondered what Fitzpatrick could possibly have wanted to add but not having seen his report or the message he had no idea. He had felt powerless to do anything about it.

The enquiry was over almost as soon as it had begun. It had taken the best part of the day. Torrance had already prepared what he wanted to say and it then followed. It was inevitable from the way in which he had conducted the enquiry how he would find the facts and rationalise his decision. Laughton was saddened to hear the word 'disobey' repeated time after time. Torrance actually paid little attention to the torn off gun panel save to suggest that it was caused by the plane diving steeply and putting unendurable pressure on the wing. His summary was that Barry had disobeyed orders; had badly executed aerobatic manoeuvres which resulted in him losing control of the plane and crashing into the ground. The accident was caused by pilot error!

They had buried Barry at St Cassian's the following week. Jessie and he had been greatly comforted by being surrounded by so many of his friends and colleagues. But their greatest comfort was having Mac with them; he having been granted compassionate leave to attend. They had thanked God that at least Mac was safe.

Chapter 23

TENBY

It had been Easter Sunday March 24th when Mac and Nell had come to him and Jessie, hand in hand and told them of their engagement to be married. They had said that they expected they would have to wait until after the War had finished before their wedding but felt they wanted to get engaged nonetheless. Both he and Jessie had been pleased. It was time that Mac settled down. It had felt such a shame that they could not have a party to celebrate but Mac had to be back with his Squadron the next day.

Then there had been Dunkirk and a week or so later the loss of Barry. Laughton had seen how hard that had hit Mac on the day he had been allowed home for his brother's funeral. He and Jessie fervently hoped that Nell's balanced character would help him come through that loss. Perhaps they would be able to spend his next pass out together but Laughton knew how difficult it had been for Mac to get one. Mac's voice spoke again to him in his mind with his own memories of those days when the loss was so acute to them all.

I did eventually get a pass out. When it came through I didn't ring home but rang Nell instead. It took ages for the operator to put me through on my trunk call to Overton Hall and it was the butler, Victor, who answered. The black Bakelite handset clunked and I imagined the butler putting it down on the oak table that stood in the hallway. I could vaguely hear voices in the background as Victor brought Nell to the telephone. Then her voice clear and sunny, spoke to me and I felt the thrill of her apparent nearness.

'Hello Mac, how are you darling?'

'I'm coping dear Nell as I hope you are. Look I am in the public phone box at the 'drome so I haven't much time. They have just given me a forty-eight hour pass. I know how you feel but won't you come to Tenby with me tomorrow just for a night together?'

'What, you mean sleep together?' she said rather directly.

'Well …… yes my love.' I said rather hesitantly and then with rather more confidence added, 'We are engaged and this is 1940!'

She told me later that she had instantly remembered the conversation she had shared only the day before with her friend Gayle who had been totally incredulous that she had not yet slept with me. 'Oh Tom and I always sleep together now when he gets any leave......... just in case, well you know.'

The seconds passed.

'What do you say? Nell please will you come with me?' I asked again now more urgently fearing that the pips would go.

The pips then began marking the end of the call.

'Yes, yes of course I will'.

'Darling I'll pick you up at 10 tomorrow ......' The telephone went dead.

Nell told me on the morrow after I had picked her up that she had been fearful of how to break the news to her parents of her going to Tenby with me. She had told herself it was her decision; that she was an adult and could make up her own mind now! The parents didn't really need to know save that she would be with me. She apparently had gone into the drawing room and was met immediately with the question.

'Was that Mac, Nellie?' Her mother had looked up from the tapestry she was working on. Mama had always called her Nellie and would not adapt to calling her Nell now that she had come of age which infuriated her! Her father continued reading the Times apparently uninterested in what was going on around him.

'Yes mama it was. He's got a forty-eight hour pass. He wants me to go with him tomorrow and stay in Tenby for a night.'

'What, at a hotel?' said her mother in the sort of tone that bore reproach.

'No, with friends mama,' she quickly invented to avoid any potential obstacle.

'Oh well that is all right now you are engaged. Just so long as there are other people around.'

'Oh there will be other people around mama!' she replied thinking of all the guests a hotel might contain in a late hot July!'

'Where does he get the petrol from; that's what I would like to know?' her father had rejoined from behind his paper, 'I can't get any these days. I suppose it's because his father is in the trade. Wish I could swan about the country like he does.'

'Oh Daddy that's not fair! Mac was telling me last week that if he wanted to he could be paid daily and do you know why?'

'I haven't a notion why Nell.'

'Because so many of our pilots are being shot down and killed, the chance of them spending the pittance they earn gets less and less. And so yes, they do get extra petrol so they can get home and see their families when they get a pass.'

'I see,' her father said in a tone that acknowledged her just rebuke, 'Well then you should go and enjoy yourself my girl,' he added more agreeably.

So it was that when I appeared next day precisely at 10am, her overnight case was in the hall and she was looking out of the window when I drove up the gravelled drive in my old red Alvis Speed Twenty. Do you remember, I bought that car in 1935 second hand and it was my pride and joy? A two door, two seater drophead coupe, it was elegance itself and had a light tan leather interior. I had intended to keep it forever!

With its two and a half litre engine by the standards of those days it was fast, very fast, with a top speed of close on ninety mph. I am pleased to say I used to drive it like the wind! There was just that once when things had gone awry. Do you remember? I had been on my way to collect a friend from Wolverhampton Station and had a minor contretemps with a traffic island. I had to telephone you, Father, to ask you to send a truck to pull me off from where I had mounted the island and got somehow stuck on the central mound! Of course, yes I had been going too fast again!

By 2pm including a short stop for a sandwich we had arrived at the hotel. I signed us in as 'Mr and Mrs H. M. Goodwin' whilst Nell stood at my side hiding her ring finger and blushing. A young man with pitch black hair parted on the right carried our two small leather overnight cases upstairs as he showed us to room 23 on the second floor. Nell explored our room which had its own bathroom and a sofa at the bottom of a large double bed which creaked a little when she sat on it to take her shoes off.

'Nell, come and look out of this window'. She pads across the carpeted floor in her stocking feet and comes over to where I am standing. Taking my outstretched hand she stands close next to me. I can feel her warmth and smell her perfume as I put my arm around her shoulder.

'Just look at that' and I point with my other hand out towards where the tang and sounds of the Irish Sea reach us as it swells its way into the shore. The view from Tenby is magnificent as we look over the bay from our window high up on the cliff. White dots in the distance out at sea mark out tiny sails and a puff of black smoke against the horizon blue, a coaler, making its slow steamy way round the coast. Beyond, I can just make out in the haze the outline of Caldey Island. Nearer inland, the bay with its sandy beach is strewn with a few trippers in swimming costumes. They are playing games with carefree children to whom the War probably seems as distant as the moon!

I turn Nell's shoulders to me and gently reaching down I cup her face in both of my hands and kiss her full on the lips. As she responds to me opening her mouth to my tongue I pull her closer to my embrace.

I know she understands how awful it has been for me these last few weeks for she has comforted me when I have openly cried tears mourning the loss of Barry.

The loss I know has taken me from her for a time, and even now, it seems from what she said on the way down she is finding it difficult sometimes to fathom my moods. Doesn't she know I am all too aware that my moods are still wildly oscillating? Away from her I feel forlornly sad but when she is with me I have managed to find peace and even a shared joy.

I still fear being killed and taken from her. If anything that has worsened in the last week or so. I know that I have been drinking more heavily as well. I have a lot on my mind and feel burdened by it all. Drink helps soften the pain of losing Barry but I know Nell can help me too. I just do not seem to be able to stop myself acting rather recklessly these days and that frightens me. Perhaps Nell being with me tonight will stop me from feeling that I cannot survive.

Our long kiss ends and she pulls away from me.

'Darling we need to talk.' she starts hesitantly.

'Do we ...... now ...... about what?' I reply feigning surprise, guessing partly what is coming.

'You are beginning to worry me ....' she continues, clearly not sure how to put what she really wants to say or that she should even say it. Perhaps she does not want to spoil this brief pass I have managed to obtain against all the odds by wrecking what is such precious time. Anyway the words seem to dry up in her throat and she stops.

'What do you mean Nell, beginning to worry you?' I stupidly rejoin.

'Oh you seem so distracted these days ....' The words are hesitantly delivered and do not seem to reflect what she wants to say but ....

'And you are surprised by that!' Unusually I feel a totally alien anger creep into my voice and although I had anticipated the exchange my emotions are somehow out of control and I explode.

'Every day instead of working with Father in the business, I am in the air in a war I never wanted, never sought but know we all must fight to stop Hitler from invading our England. It has cost my brother and so many of my pals their lives and you worry that I seem to be distracted!'

I suddenly feel tears prick at my eyes and on impulse she moves to take me in her arms no doubt to envelope me in her warmth to calm me. But I am still full of fury and I push her away as if suddenly in my vulnerability I cannot bear her close. The happiness of the moment is lost to both of us.

'I need to go for a walk,' I say and leave the room, childishly banging the door behind me.

She told me later that evening how she had shed tears herself after I had gone and had sat down again on the double bed dabbing at her wet eyes with her hankie as she castigated herself for handling the situation so badly. She said that she had realised that she had been foolish; should have thought it through better, and chosen her words more carefully. She eventually had gone into the bathroom, washed her face and refreshed her lipstick. That had made her feel better. She then had stood by the window from where she could see me purposely pacing down the beach away from the hotel smoking a cigarette. I had bought some from a tobacconist opposite the hotel having left my silver cigarette case; you know the one bearing the monogram on the table in our room. Back there, she had taken one of the Piccadilly cigarettes out of the case, lit it with an onyx table lighter and exhaling a plume of smoke, she had sat down to watch over the bay for me, feeling wretched and wishing for me to return.

I did not return until the sun had fallen behind passing cloud and shadows had started to herald the evening sky. My anger by then was long since spent and we said 'sorry' to each other. Neither of us ventured further into where we had been, fearing perhaps that to do so would waste even more of the precious leave before I had to return to Middle Wallop. So we took the red Alvis and drove out to a pub overlooking the sea, a little further up the coast. With a gin-n-it in her hand and me with a pint of the local bitter, we sat outside watching the sunset.

As the sun dipped into the sea at its horizon and the pinks turned to burnished scarlet I relaxed and took her hand in mine. We sat for a long time in silent companionship until just deepened blues remained at the line where sky and sea merged. Then we talked and set what had happened earlier aside. By the time we left the pub we were back to the joyfulness of where we had been when I had picked her up from Overton Hall that morning. Our conversation as ever, ranged now over so many topics that I think we were left with a feeling of breathlessness at our attempt to cover everything and everyone which, or who needed to be included!

Dinner back at the hotel was constrained by the rationing but the woman who managed it while her husband was away in the Army came to us at our table. She said that they had been able to buy from the harbour fishermen some fresh mackerel caught that day, so we both ordered and enjoyed that with some local vegetables followed by some tinned pears. The hotel even managed to rustle up a bottle of white wine which was delicious. I think it was a Chateau bottled white burgundy. It certainly brought us to reminisce and back to our enjoyment once again of just being together. Eventually we finished our coffee and tired by the emotions of the day we journeyed to bed in an excited expectation of finding each other between the sheets.

In the bedroom I go to her. Wrapping my arms around her I hold her tight. I feel now as happy as I had done earlier in the day when I had first collected her. I kiss her tiny kisses over her face making her smile and then laugh. She seems to want me more then than ever before. So I take her by her hand. I notice her finger, still wearing the sparkle of my ring. I start to undress her button by button but suddenly with a wanting urgency of desire she is taking off my jacket and then my shirt as if the removal of my clothing will slough off the emotional wounds I have suffered and naked I can be myself and hers again.

Nell is now in just her bra and panties as my hands more searching now, reach for the clasp and release her beautifully formed small breasts to my hands. As her bra falls to the floor I gradually kneel in front of her, kissing tiny kisses to her bare neck and then across her chest as I do so. My lips fall onto her breasts and I suckle her nipples making them erect and hard. She moans with ecstatic pleasure and becomes wild as I make love to her. She leans down and pulls her panties off herself as if feeling the intensity of desire warming her there. Now I am at last naked too and pressing my hardness against her. We both breathe with greater urgency as she pulls me onto the bed on top of her. She wants me.

I can wait no longer as I feel my moistness next to her. The centre of her being seems to scream for me and she writhes underneath me until I can feel my hard tip next to her. She throws her arms out to her sides.

'Mac, Mac come inside me ......NOW!' she shouts to me in passion. She takes hold of me and guides me inside her until I am part of her in a warm closeness and am thrusting deeper and deeper into her holding her under her bottom with my hands and kissing her passionately and wantonly on her mouth. We have both now passed beyond any point of return. It is as if we are hurtling towards an edge and my thinking is lost to time and space.

'Take me Mac...... I am all yours my darling......'

'Wait for me, wait for me ......'

'Come to me Mac I want you.'

'Oh take me now my love, my dearest love, I am all yours too' ...... and with joy we cling to each other at that moment when our passage together over the edge is fulfilled and we fall into the most brilliant blissful light as one being.

Minutes pass. Eventually we lie side by side for a while talking and recovering.

'Oh Nell, my darling Nell, my beautiful English rose ...... that was unbelievable.'

I lit a couple of cigarettes and passed one to Nell who took it gratefully inhaling its smoke. We leant against big cushions of pillows and smoked our cigarettes as we chatted. Then before they were finished I stubbed them out so that she could snuggle up to me resting her head on my right shoulder and putting her leg across my body. I slipped my arm about her and my hand lazily stroked her hair. I had never experienced such emotional closeness with a girl before. Was this really how it was between couples? How lucky they were. This is how I wanted to spend the rest of my life. With Nell. In bed! The thought made me laugh and then she made me tell why!

We rested now, the dark of the room folding around us until I heard her breathing regularly and knew she was asleep. I smiled to myself in sheer happiness that at last she had been able to give herself to me completely.

His eldest son had never had secrets from him but Mac sharing such intimacies had surprised even embarrassed him! Aloud to the empty glade as if Mac were there with him he had entreated.

'Tell me about Aldertag Day, Mac when the Luftwaffe thought they would break our resistance by taking out the RAF's ability to respond to attack. Don't expect you know it by that name but you will know the day I mean, 13th August 1940.'

Chapter 24

ALDERTAG DAY

Mac's voice though had faded to silence and no immediate answers came. Laughton recalled then that it was on the first day of the Court of Enquiry at Drem into Barry's accident that news had come from Mac that 609 Squadron was moving their base from Northolt to Warmwell in Dorset. It had all made sense to him. The Home Guard had been put on alert and the intelligence he had been made privy to was that the Germans were planning an invasion. They would need air superiority to achieve that without huge losses if they were going to bridge the Channel. So the South of England's defences would have to be put out of action. The Luftwaffe would surely bomb the air defences based there.

Mac's move with 609 turned out to be all a bit of a kerfuffle! Apparently there were orders which were then countermanded until they were eventually ordered to move to Middle Wallop to be with 238 Squadron. He had never quite understood how Warmwell then came into it but it seemed as if the Squadron somehow then covered it on a rotation with 152 Squadron based there permanently.

They were soon in action and the air battle which later had been called the Battle of Britain had effectively started just a few days after Mac had moved.

Suddenly Mac's voice breaks impatiently in on his own memories and at once takes over his train of thought.

After our new CO, George Darley arrived our general depression lifted as he took control. Everything was tightened up and at last someone with experience of battle was teaching us the knack of survival in the air. His intensive training programme kept us in the air day after day. We tried mock attacks of every sort with Darley taking the part of the enemy. Out of the sun and taking us by surprise in every way, his flying skills were so much more sophisticated than ours but he was determined that the Squadron would become a fully fledged fighting machine. Our kill to loss ratio at last started to change and we became hardened professionals rather than amateur friends. By the 12th we had flown several ops and lost a few of our pilots. But we were at last pasting the enemy!

We were scrambled that morning as a large formation of twin engine, Ju 88 bombers had been spotted in our sector. I was flying Spitfire K9997 as 'Red Two' wing man to Frank Howell. Sgt Feary was the third member of our Section. Darley had put us together as part of 'A' Flight when we were still back at Northolt and we stayed together after that. We also had Green Section of 'B' Flight alongside us that day.

Flying at about 23,000 feet over Portsmouth and the Isle of Wight that day we spot them beneath us. They had already been attacking Portsmouth and Ventnor. Their activities were protectively ringed by circling escorts which included Messerschmitt Bf 110s.

On Howell's signal 'A' Flight leads the attack against the Me. 110s diving to scatter the enemy planes each of us intent on picking off at least one of them and destroying it. This is how we had planned attacks in training with one Flight leading and scattering leaving the other Flight to destroy and kill. We catch them totally unawares. I pick out an Me. 110 on the edge of the protective ring and before he knows it I am on his tail. Then he is in range.

I press the fire button. My first burst of bullets is high and misses, goes straight over the top of him. He now knows I am behind him and starts to turn tightly but I am ready for that and follow him. The Messerschmitt is no match for my Spitfire in manoeuvrability. I am closing on him fast. I am very close now and can see some tracer from his rear gunner smoke-trail the air to my left as he starts turning to the right. Another longer burst. This time smoke starts to plume from his fuselage. Before he can fully change course I get yet another burst in and am rewarded this time by seeing flames bursting from his wings.

He starts to spin and I am somehow aware of the pilot and gunner trying to get out of the cockpit but then having fallen a few hundred feet the plane explodes below me and they do not make it. I have no time for even a tinge of regret. The adrenalin and Darley's training keeps me focussed. Darley has brought 'B' Flight into the attack and various dog fights are going on all over the sky. I am back in the thick of the battle raging with the other Messerschmitts and Junkers all of whom are now desperately trying to escape across the Channel back to their bases in France.

We are outnumbered several times over but we have done the job. We land back at Middle Wallop. 'Bags of Joy?' as the ground crew always used to ask on our return is answered by me in the affirmative today! But looking at my port wing I can see several holes from the bullets taken in battle. She will need extensive repair before she is fit to fly again. The ground crew muster some help to get her over to one of the hangars while I go off to make my claim for my first kill. It is confirmed by McArthur of 'B' Flight who saw my Me.110 go down. The Squadron has bagged something like six Messerschmitts. It is my first kill and I feel at last I have started to avenge Barry's death in some way.

On the morrow, Tuesday 13th August, we fly down to Warmwell. K9997 is still being repaired so I am once again flying N3024 with my call sign PR-H. The day is pretty miserable with low cloud cover and we do not expect to be scrambled. Nothing comes through from Group so we just sit about in the tents at Dispersal playing cards and losing money! We are all pretty fed up! But the weather starts to clear a bit in the afternoon and visibility improves. I am just drinking a cup of tea when the scramble bell sounds. Typical! I run out to the hide where Don and Tommy with a couple of other ground crew have been checking over my Spitfire. Fortunately, nothing major needed to be done and they are just gathering up their tools and paint when I arrive breathless. They quickly help me up onto the wing and into the cockpit. The starter batteries are as ever ready and quickly plugged in to start my Merlin. The engine coughs once, splutters some oily exhaust fumes over the ground crew and then is in full roaring mood!

I take off with Red Section and we are in the air easily within the target of two minutes from scramble being sounded. Altogether a force of about thirteen of us – very appropriate I think for today is the 13th after all! We patrol over Lyme Bay at about 15.000 feet. Red Leader has commanded radio silence. I look over in his direction and see him indicate with his hand. At the same time I hear distinctive German voices coming over the radio! To the south of where we are in the direction which Howell has indicated and well below us I can see a large formation of enemy aircraft in separate 'v' shaped groups. Over to my right I spot another similar formation flying in the direction of Southampton. Stepped above both droning formations I can see a large escort of Me 110s and Me 109s. We are spoilt for choice!

The Skipper though has instantly decided to go for the first group which seems to be heading in the direction we have just flown from, Middle Wallop itself. Perhaps that is his reason. I must remember to ask him when we land.

We plunge through the sky and as we close up on the group of fifty or more planes I realise that they are Ju. 87s, 'Stukas'. They are sitting ducks! Bags of joy! We follow the same attack pattern as the previous day but this time Darley and 'B' Flight first and then Howell with 'A' Flight second to do the real damage. As we cut into them I have my guns blazing at a Stuka that drifts off to the left and starts going down with thick white smoke billowing from its fuselage.

Another is now in my path. I fire a long burst into him and then as he spirals out of control in flames I am through the group and into empty sky. I loop as the Me. 109s try to grapple with the Squadron but I can see other enemy planes going down. I see a Me. 109 go down into the sea after he was taken out by David Crook. I will be able to confirm that one at least. I can see several parachutes falling towards the sea so we shall have more prisoners to feed when they are picked up! Still, not my problem!

The whole German attack has been thwarted. The planes which have survived and they still outnumber those we have taken out, have turned for France and are disappearing into cloud now. We do not have the operational capacity to chase after them. Radio silence is broken by Howell.

'Well done chaps. Let's go home and have some tea!'

It's all a game isn't it? I land back at Warmwell and report my successes before writing up my log. Then I go in search of the others who have taken part in the day's sport in what passes as the Mess Bar. We are all on good form and cock-a-hoop! We have come through the combat unscathed, as have our planes save one lightly damaged. It turns out that in a four minute swoop we have destroyed no less than ten Stukas. We have even bagged four of the Messerschmitt escorts.

One of the pilots who did not take part in the sport offers to take a group photograph of us all. So we all go outside whilst it is still daylight and stand as a group near one of the tents whilst he takes a photograph of us. The blackboard that normally just shows our order of take off now shows against our names the victories we have claimed. I go over with Appleby and Staples to have a closer look. I see I have been credited correctly with my two 87's. Not bad for four minutes work!

Then Novi strikes up on the piano and we all take our pints over to be near him and the evening passes to the raucous singing of various rugby songs and other ditties! I don't make it back to bed until well after eleven hoping that the enemy will get up a bit later next day!

Chapter 25

14TH AUGUST 1940

The next day fortunately turns out to be cloudy. My head feels a bit muzzy as well! The Squadron flies back from Warmwell to Middle Wallop at 0700 hours. Several of the Spits including mine need minor repairs to various bullet holes collected yesterday so we don't return those to the hides but park them up in a line near the hangars where the ground crew can get at them more easily. They are a bit vulnerable parked up here but I don't think further raids are expected today in our sector. The ceiling today is very low. I would think the highest it has been is about three hundred feet. There have been no reports of enemy activity from Group.

It is almost as if yesterday had not happened. The jubilation has dissipated. Today is a complete anti-climax. We are all hanging around near the planes in our kit ready to scramble, very disconsolate that we can't have another go at them. Some enterprising soul has brought some of the Lloyd Loom chairs and the gramophone up from the Bungalow we have been using as our HQ, at Middle Wallop. Harbour Lights is one of the 78s we play and play. I smile hearing Vera Lynn sing 'I long to hold you near and kiss you just once more. But you were on the ship and I was on the shore' .... and I think of lovely Nell.

I play pontoon with Novi. I win a bit of money off him before lunch which he promptly regains after! Some of the others are also playing cards or draughts or just sitting in their chairs trying to nap, reading or smoking cigarettes.

It's five o'clock in the afternoon. The balloon suddenly goes up! We have had absolutely no warning from sector HQ save that there had been an earlier air raid in the Southampton area when thick cloud had prevented the intruders being identified. Novi and I have just lit up again when I hear them; no room for mistake; it's the distinct throbbing sound of Junker engines. We all leap into activity even before anyone calls for us to scramble. I grab my silver cigarette case and the remainder of my kit and run towards my plane dragging my flying helmet on over my head.

It is complete mayhem. They have caught us totally by surprise. Men are running to take cover in the slip trenches and to man the ack-ack. I see three ground crew, two of whom I know rush over to No 5 Hangar. They start to shut the doors to protect the two Spitfires being overhauled inside. The steel doors are massive but slowly they are closing.

The skipper calls to us to get aloft. We need no second bidding. I am sprinting to where my plane is parked, armed and ready to go. Some of the ground crew recognise our intention. They run to help us get the chocks away and airborne quickly. I hear the whine of the first of the bombs. Over to my left, one bursts through the roof of No 5. The explosion that follows lifts one of the hangar's huge doors off its rails and it falls. The chaps trying to close it cannot get out of its way. I hear muffled screams as it crushes them. They didn't stand a chance. Flames are already flickering from inside No 5 by the time I reach my plane seconds later. I see that a few others have also reached their planes. I recognise Crook and John Dundas amongst them.

Bombs are now falling all around us. Pits are beginning to form in the recently repaired runway. The fire engine and ambulance's bells are ringing as they tear towards the hangar. Then the ack-ack starts up not before time. Whether they actually can see any of their targets I doubt. We need to get into the air whilst we still have planes to fly and room to take off.

Tubby has managed to reach my plane. Don and Tommy arrive as I do but they are out of breath. Tubby helps me on with my chute and lifejacket and then gives me a leg-up onto the wing. I slide myself into the already open cockpit. I close the hood, connect my oxygen; plug in the R/T and buckle my harness before switching on. The Merlin fires first time as I give the thumbs up to Tommy who is operating the starter batteries. He pulls out the plug from the engine. Don and Tubby pull away the chocks. I taxi quickly to join 'A' Flight.

Over the intercom comes the voice of Frank Howell. It is instantly reassuring and calming. 'Red leader to flight. Let's get up there after them chaps!' He sounds just as he does when he is taking 'A' Flight up for training exercises! We don't wait for clearance from the Tower or further orders. There is no time for formalities. I glance quickly at the windsock. The three of us taxi together and take off into the wind. I don't know if any of the other squadrons manage to get off behind us but as I turn with the Flight I look back and see other bombs exploding rendering the grass runway useless.

I climb steeply. Soon I am engulfed by cloud. Flight leader orders us to fly a bearing that swings us towards the coast. I lose visual contact with the others. Over the radio I hear 'Blue leader, Junkers at three o'clock'. I recognise the CO's voice so I know that 'B' Flight has also managed to get into the air. Still immersed in heavy cloud I can't see a blind thing! I am trying to remain calm despite the rush of excitement. I feel angry. Why the hell hadn't these planes been spotted earlier heading our way? Why hadn't the coastal radar picked them up? Where are the rest of the Flight? Nothing further comes over the radio.

Then suddenly I am out of the cloud and the sun is bright. The line of the coast is visible below. My eyes adjust. Immediately I see a couple of Junkers to my left about 150' below me. I don't think they have seen me. I decide to attack and push the stick forward and slightly to port to dive. The Merlin is roaring as I make my charge across the sky. It's inevitable they'll eventually see me but I don't care so long as I get to them first. Yes, they have seen me. They are bursting away from each other. I am going after the one diving towards the coast.

I bear down on him. My right thumb covers the 'fire button'. I am in range. He is within my sights. Now! I let off a quick burst. I see sparks and a bit of smoke. He turns tightly to avoid me. Some of the shells strike his starboard wing tip. Damn missed the bugger! I turn too feeling the G force almost swamp me as I expect the old girl to do the impossible, but we get round. He is still in my sights. I close again. He is back within range. I unleash a longer burst this time. I see it smash into his fuselage. A ball of fire and black smoke appear in front of me. He explodes. He falls out of the sky. I must have hit his fuel tanks.

I roar through the pall of black smoke left hanging there. Suddenly I am aware of another plane. It's dead astern. It's a 109! Damn! Absorbed in attack I had not spotted the escort. In the millisecond I take to identify him my plane shudders as she is hit. Then he is gone. Has one of the others seen him and taken him out? I have no time to guess or find out. My plane is going down. The controls are no longer responding. They feel heavy. Something is badly wrong. I am not going to be able to land her. Is that smoke coming from the engine? Christ she's on fire. I need to get out and fast. The sea is just over there. Oh help I am still over houses! My best chance is to bale out over the sea. If I come down here I will be killed. Worse, so will a lot of others!

I manage to pull her round. She is heading out to sea. I pull the canopy back. It jams. I pull a bit harder. My left arm is throbbing and I am beginning to feel faint. There is a red stain on my sleeve. I don't have time. I must get this canopy open. There, it's back at last. Why can't I lever myself up? My left arm has no power. The reality hits me. I am bleeding badly from a shoulder wound. My plane is tilting and starting to gradually die towards the waves below. I must get out. I must! I pull the stick over hard. This is desperate. The old girl responds one last time. As I unplug my R/T and oxygen and release my harness I feel her roll. I manage to tip myself out. The feeling of faintness is stronger.

The air is more immediate now as it rushes past. Its cold braces me back to reality. I reach down with my right hand. Where is my ripcord? Got it! I pull and there is a sharp jerk as I am suddenly supported and floating down towards the sea. I can see the old girl now in flames spinning down below me faster and gathering speed. She hits the waves which spume around her in a steamy maelstrom for a moment and then she is gone forever from my sight. Over to my right is a pier and I can just see people like upright matchsticks moving there. I hope they have seen me! I brace myself ready for my inevitable impact with the water. Oh mother I wish you were here now to pick me up as you used to when I was a child! I hit the water and my chute's silk canopy lies just beyond me like a crumpled bed sheet.

The water is cold, very cold. The swell of the blue-green waves is daunting. I feel I am being pulled out to sea. In this trough I am being chilled alive! Thank God for my Mae West. It inflated when I hit the water and it's keeping me afloat. If I could just get my sodding flying boots off I could at least try and swim with my right arm. I can't be that far from the shore. The shock of the cold water has stopped my arm throbbing. I can't feel it now let alone move it. I feel so weak; my teeth are chattering as I fight this deep cold. Surely they must have seen me come down. Why aren't they out here rescuing me? Where are they? I vaguely hear an engine. I try to shout but I don't seem to have any voice.

Minutes, that feel like hours, elapse as I drift amongst the waves. I can't hear that engine now. I did hear it. I am sure I heard it. The sound seems to have faded and gone away. Am I going to die? I feel so faint now. I just want to sleep! No I must try and hang on, hang on. They will find me, they must. Oh Mother, Father, dearest Betty...... Barry, dear Barry, stay with me now...... Our Father which art in heaven ...... hallowed be Thy name...... Thy Kingdom come ...... Thy will be done......"

Chapter 26

AFTERMATH

And then he can no longer hear Mac's voice in his mind, speaking to him. Laughton's eyes mist over yet again as he recalled the telegram arriving at Palmers Hill. It had been the second telegram from the War Office in two months. Its delivery had interrupted breakfast in the morning room. What silly details you remember. He was eating his second piece of toast and marmalade! He could still remember those dire typed capitals:

'REGRET TO INFORM YOU FLYING OFFICER NO 90269 GOODWIN REPORTED MISSING 14TH AUGUST STOP THIS DOES NOT NECESSARILY MEAN EITHER KILLED OR WOUNDED STOP'.

There had been no reassurance for him in those words. Yet he had realised that hope was still alive in him. He received the telegram at the front door and had returned to Jessie in the morning room with a heavy heart to tell her.

Then there had been the long days, and even longer nights without news. Day after day dragged past interminably as they hoped for the best, fearing the worst! He had gained snippets of information from Mac's Squadron. He recalled one of Mac's ground crew, a chap who had called himself 'Tubby', had told him how they had waited for hour after hour in vain for Mac to return to Middle Wallop. He was the only one who had honestly said he feared the worst.

Gradually all realistic hope died within him and Jessie despite the many letters and cards of support friends and colleagues of Mac had sent. And then on the twenty-eighth of August came that last telegram. They had found his body given up by the sea to a beach on the Isle of Wight near Yarmouth.

It was amazing how hope stayed alive in you until the certainty of loss. At least there had then been a sense of an end to it all and some relief but no comfort. The loss had finally annihilated his dreams of being succeeded in his business by Mac. So much emotional investment had been laid waste by the boys' premature deaths. He felt that Jessie had found it even harder than him and that was devastating enough. She had been closer to the boys than him. After all she had

126

been the one who had been at home caring for the family while he had built up a successful business enterprise to support them all.

He recalled when that second telegram had arrived how his success had seemed in comparison to all that Jessie had done, so very hollow. He had fervently wished he had spent more time with both Mac and Barry when they were children and shared their childish joys and sorrows. He recalled how he had, in effect, repeated the neglect of his own father. Now as he sat alone in the glade he mused on how he had lost both his boys and borne the guilt and the pain for a decade.

Jessie had gone to her desk in the drawing room later that morning and brought a letter to him as he sat motionless in his Gun Room. They were both in the agony of loss. She had handed it to him to open and to read. The envelope was in Mac's elegant flowing handwriting and addressed in black ink to his mother with the additional inscription 'To be opened in the event of my death'.

'No Jessie!' he had said rather harshly, 'Mac wrote this for you. You should at least honour his memory by opening it yourself.'

With hindsight his own distress had been so acute that he had hidden behind insensitivity when he should have been so much gentler. His reply had obviously hurt, for Jessie was yet again in tears and he had had to fight his own back too.

'Laughton dearest, I can't. Please help me. You open it and read it to me.'

He had taken the envelope back from her. Reaching forward he opened the top drawer in his desk and extracted his silver paper knife. Very carefully and deliberately he had inserted its point into the top and slit it open. He removed the single folded sheet that lay inside and unfolded it.

His throat caught as he began to read. He coughed to clear it. Jessie had reached forward and placed her hand on his arm. He started to read aloud and was comforted by the letter's opening address.

My dearest Mother and Father,

I am proud to write you this letter, because if you are reading it, it will mean that I will have done my bit for the Old Country and all that we hold dear to us. I pray God that others will carry on where I have failed until victory is won.

Life at Palmers Hill with you has always been exciting and you have always sought to give us all that we could have possibly have desired. I want you to know how much I love you all. I am not afraid of dying. After all I will be again with Barry from whom separation has been so very painful. I have also lost several dear friends from Worcestershire already. Try not to mourn me for too long. I will have died in a worthy cause. I have left a letter for my dear Nell for my Squadron to send if I am lost. Give my best love to my beautiful and dear sister, Betty. I hope she will meet someone who will make her happy. Remember me always.

Your devoted son,
Mac

He recalled the silence which had followed after he had read the contents aloud to Jessie. He had stood, and she had come to him, taken the letter and read it once again to herself. She had wept and wept and he had then put his arms around her and just held her head to his chest until his shirt was wet with her tears but he still held her. He was frightened of what she would think if she saw him break down in front of her and he had fought back the tears that moistened his own eyes.

Chapter 27

MAC'S FUNERAL

Was it really only nine weeks before when he and Jessie had alighted from another similar black polished limousine behind another hearse? Only nine weeks since Mac had flown his Spitfire up from RAF Northolt and executed a victory roll over his brother's grave the evening of the day they had buried Barry. How a few weeks could alter lives forever?

This time though it was different. This time it brought finality to the dreams he had had for his boys. There would be no heir for the family, for another generation of Goodwins to take his name on; no one to take over the reins of the business he had put together; no boy to enjoy gallops with across the green fields awash with early morning dew near Palmers Hill.

The RAF bearer party of NCOs from a midland station; the name of which was never disclosed for security reasons, were removing Mac's coffin bearing the Union Flag from the hearse parked by the lych-gate to St. Cassian's. A group of villagers stood solemnly on the opposite side of the road. He could hear some of the women openly crying. He recalled being touched by their presence which somehow had lifted his spirit on that dread occasion.

As the six RAF men in dress uniform wearing white gloves had raised Mac to their shoulders to bear him towards the church he had put his hand in Jessie's. She had an already wet handkerchief to her eyes as her tears flowed without respite and he bit his lower lip to hold his own firmly in check. She took his hand and held it tightly. Betty was on his other side; they both emotionally were in tatters. He put his arm round Betty and then took her hand as well. Both his women wore black as he did himself but the detail of their dresses was no part of the memory.

The Vicar of Stone, Harry Bailey, came over to them and seeing that his hands were both taken up, had not sought to shake his hand but nodded with a wan smile muttering something that no doubt had been appropriate but instantly forgettable. The three of them had quietly moved to be behind the coffin and then slowly the small procession had moved in silence up the winding path to the Church accompanied only by the sound of the tolling of the single bell from the tower and the sound of orders from the Sergeant in charge of the bearers.

129

As they entered the Church porch Nell was waiting to join them. She had obviously been weeping but was trying hard to be brave. Betty had taken Nell's hand in hers and fallen in behind him and Jessie as they had entered the Church itself to the sound of the organ playing Chopin's March Funebre. He had heard the congregation rise to their feet and the Vicar start to read the Sentences as the coffin was borne and placed on the oak trestles near to the steps leading to the Choir.

'I am the resurrection and the life,' saith the Lord; 'he that believeth in me, though he were dead, yet shall he live: and whosoever liveth and believeth in me shall never die,' and: 'I know that my Redeemer liveth …'

They were ushered into front pews and he had tried to say a prayer but the words would not come! Behind them he could almost feel the wave of comfort flowing towards them. He had noticed that they were all there; the family in strength; Viscountess Cobham, her daughters, Audrey and Lavinia, staff from the works; many others in uniform, Army and RAF. The Church was packed. He felt somehow numb and detached from what was happening around him. He had picked up the Order of Service sheet that had awaited his arrival in the pew. It had been so carefully and lovingly compiled by Jessie and Betty. He had sung the hymns, kneeled and mouthed the prayers and listened whilst Mac was remembered by his friends in words and music but his mind was elsewhere.

The words of Mac's last letter had kept going through his mind. 'If you are reading it, it will mean that I will have done my bit for the Old Country and all that we hold dear to us. I pray God that others will carry on where I have failed until victory is won'. The boys had been so so different. Barry full of 'go' and energy hardly stopping for a moment to see the wider pictures in life through fear of missing a moment of exhilaration in one of his exploits; Mac, always thoughtful and caring of how his actions would impact on the family, even to the end.

He recalled all these thoughts and many more had passed through his mind before his reverie had been brought to a sudden end by the bearer party collecting Mac's light oak coffin from where it lay atop the trestles with his Service dress cap on top together with the family wreath of white gladioli grown at Palmers Hill. The organist started to play Handel's The Dead March from 'Saul'.

The Church's warm comforting feel was suddenly replaced by the snap of cold breezy autumnal air as they passed outside and made their solemn way, as they had just those few weeks ago, to where the horse-chestnut was now beginning to shed its leaves already forming a pall over Barry's grave. The earth was still brown, and some of the wreaths still lay against the mound in various states of decay. Now there would be two side by side. The anguish within him wanted him to scream and as he fought it he focussed so that it did not turn to tears.

To the left hand side of Barry's grave there now lay open a further grave surrounded with moss, maidenhair fern and asters. An RAF bugler stood adjacent to the grave. The burial party set the coffin down on slats of wood which had been laid across the top of the grave. White ropes were passed under the coffin and the bearers waited. The area was now packed with all the mourners from the Church. The Vicar dressed in his white surplice paused until everyone had gathered. He had heard few of the opening words of prayer as he had placed his arms around Jessie and Betty standing now close to him and weeping openly.

'We therefore commit his body to the ground; earth to earth, ashes to ashes, dust to dust; in the sure and certain hope of the Resurrection to eternal life.'

The words struck him deeply and he too could no longer hold back the tears that brimmed full his eyes, and flowed then down his cheeks, until Jessie reached across with the handkerchief she was still clutching and tried to wipe them away.

The Vicar ushered them forward. In turn they each had sprinkled a trowel full of earth into the grave. As he looked down for the last time the pristine brass plaque dazzled him as the sun's rays struck it momentarily through a gap in the overhanging tree. Then it was done. The bugler sounded the 'Last Post'. Three volleys of shots were fired into the air. It was over.

In the Swan afterwards he endured the reception that was called for on such occasions to support those who had travelled a distance. It was another hour before the three of them had been able to escape back to Palmers Hill and be with their memories of the boys within its quietude. He recalled how as the limousine had turned into the driveway and up the drive where the boys had once played so happily it had started to rain, as if his own tears of grief were matched by the heavens.

Chapter 28

MEETING RADFORD AGAIN

It had not been until much later after the War had ended in the later 1940s that he had met Radford again. He had happened to be at the RAF Club in Piccadilly with a friend who was working at the Air Ministry. Still in uniform he had seen Radford sitting on his own in the bar drinking a cup of coffee and reading the Times. Laughton had noticed that the uniform rings on his sleeve suggested that he was now a Wing Commander. Back in 1940 he had been a Flight Lieutenant. He had clearly done well in the intervening years.

Laughton had gone over to him to say 'hello'. Radford had turned from his paper, smiled and risen courteously to his feet and shaken him by the hand. He had remembered Laughton instantly. Soon they had been joined by Laughton's friend. It turned out that he had served sometime under Radford and they too recognised each other. The usual pleasantries over, he recalled how it was Radford who had deliberately turned the conversation to the Enquiry and the way it had been conducted.

Radford had seemed to want to unburden himself about what had really happened. He was unstintingly frank in telling Laughton not only about Group Captain Torrance's background, but also about the way in which he was completely prejudiced. Laughton had listened quietly and found his own opinions formed at the time being firmly confirmed.

Squadron Leader Brian Torrance who had been given charge of the Enquiry had been forty plus and past active service. His service career had been mainly spent in administration. He was based at RAF Kinross. He had little practical experience of flying aircraft although he had flown a few of the bi-planes in the twenties and thirties. He was then in charge of servicing aircraft for No 8 Group. It was a somewhat tedious job even for someone who had spent a lifetime doing tedious jobs for an administration that had high expectations. He had thought he was badly underpaid and carried that resentment into everything that he did.

The first Group Captain who had been asked to conduct the enquiry had been too ill and had been forced to decline, so by default, Torrance had been brought in as a substitute. Apparently, when Torrance was telephoned and asked to 'stand in' to conduct a fatal accident enquiry involving a Hurricane he had jumped at the chance. Although there was not much that he did not know about the mechanics of Hurricanes it seemed that his real purpose in accepting the task was that it might mean a few days away from the tedium.

Radford related what Torrance had said to him about that initial telephone call. It seemed to have been intentionally and clearly laced with incantation. Torrance had been told that although it was a matter entirely for him, the pilot, whoever he was, seemed to have been the author of his own misfortune; nothing had been found wrong with the plane! But Torrance needed no such encouragement. Planes to him were sacred; pilots came and went!

Torrance had read the RAF Casualty Card by the time of Radford's briefing and had told Radford that the important bit on the Card was that there was no suggestion of plane failure or of any ground crew errors. He had boasted to Radford that he had never had any complaint relating to an accident which he had not been able to deal with effectively.

Most of the accidents he had previously dealt with in his view had been caused by simple pilot error. Anyway, he had said, it was bad for morale if the planes or ground crew came in for stick. By the time he had spent twenty minutes briefing Torrance prior to the enquiry it had appeared to Radford that Torrance felt that the accident could easily be put down by him to pilot error.

Radford had been utterly appalled. Torrance's mind appeared to have been made up long before he had heard any of the evidence. He had declined the sherry that Torrance had offered him in the Mess and left in disgust. The matter had troubled him then and later. Only now that the War had ended and he had met Laughton again in different circumstances did he feel able to unburden himself of his disgust at the way matters had been handled.

Laughton had at long last also been able to ask what the message from the engineer had said. Radford had told him that it had asked for him to be recalled as he thought one aspect of what he had said needed to be altered. Fitzpatrick had later told him that after giving his evidence he had gone back to the wreck of L2115 to have another look at the remnants of the port wing.

On minute examination he had found something which he had missed during his first examination, the day following the accident. The gun panel was clearly missing as he had noted. The wing had been badly mangled by the impact and twisted by the subsequent fire. But when he examined the rear internal sockets into which the fastenings fitted he had found distortion marks. They suggested that the panel had not been torn away suddenly but that it had taken a prolonged period of some seconds before it had finally come adrift. The one on the starboard wing was still held secure by its special fastenings but at least one was not properly tightened.

He had concluded that the port gun panel must have been gradually torn away during one of the stalled turns that Barry had carried out, or the resultant spinning that ensued according to the boy witness. If so, it would have braked the port wing sufficiently to make the resultant spin much more difficult for the pilot to control. Had Fitzpatrick been recalled he would have said that the drag on the wing would have been much greater and for longer a time than he had suggested in evidence. The pilot would have had great difficulty in controlling the spin or spins. Once the spinning was corrected there would have been less time to come out of the dive.

The loose fastening on the starboard wing indicated that whoever had last refitted the gun panels probably had not fixed them down correctly. He had also looked at the relevant Air Ministry's Air Publication the text of which seemed to indicate categorically that from the height Barry had started his manoeuvre he would not have had sufficient altitude to regain level flight after a prolonged correction of the spin. If the gun panel had not come adrift in that manner then Barry would have certainly corrected the spin almost immediately and not crashed at all.

Had that further evidence been accepted as correct then the findings of the enquiry, in Radford's opinion, would have been different. He, himself had been satisfied by it, that it had been ground crew error, and not the pilot that had caused the fatal accident.

When Laughton realised that Barry had been unnecessarily blamed he had felt angry. True Barry ought not to have been doing stall turns but with his flying skill he would have emerged unscathed had the plane not let him down. Radford had apologised for telling him what had happened in such detail fearing it would cause Laughton distress. He had not been distressed though. Despite his anger it felt as if Barry had been vindicated. He had indeed thanked Radford when they had parted for his frankness and had told him that he would always be welcome to visit them at Palmers Hill, if he ever found himself in the Midlands.

Chapter 29

A DOWNHILL SLOPE

Once he had known that Barry had been wrongly blamed for the accident that had cost him his life, Laughton had found it difficult to find any activity or indeed anything that could lift his mood. He reflected that the reality was that nothing had really interested him or caught his imagination after he had lost the boys. He felt he had tried, God knows, in all honesty, he had tried!

He had thrown himself into the Home Guard and been appointed Lieutenant-Colonel to command the 10th Battalion of the Worcesters. But neither that interest nor Betty's wedding at St Saviour's in October 1944 to Bob Walker, an RAF officer, had regenerated his interest in living. Even the joy of having two young grandsons around at Palmers Hill had been muted by what had seemed to be a never-ending depressive mood.

In fact collecting his memories together now, he realised he had not been able to escape the loneliness and isolation he felt at being separated from his boys. The devastation of the loss they had all suffered in 1940, he still felt with the intensity of present anguish. He had not been able to absorb the loss and move on. Jessie and Betty, somehow more stoic than him, had been able to get what had happened into some sort of proud perspective and turn the page. Whilst he had admired their fortitude he had not been able to emulate them.

Day after day, week after week and as the months rolled into years following Mac's funeral, he had found himself being drawn to the graves even before the white Portland stone headstones were erected and the many flowers had been cleared away. He recalled how he had so frequently driven over in the Plymouth and walked up to the graves oblivious of the weather. Often he had been soaked by rain, save when the horse chestnut had been in leaf and had protected him.

He had simply wanted to be near them. He had wanted to tell them so many things he should have shared with them. All of it on reflection boiled down to him wanting to tell them just how much he had loved them; something he had not been able to express to them during their lives. He now so deeply regretted that he had not been able to muster the words.

Sometimes he would tell Jessie where he had been; other times not. At least they went together on birthdays and at Christmas to lay flowers on both graves.

But she had her own grief to bear and he had been sensitive to her burden. She in turn seemed unable to comfort him despite their closeness in the past; unable to reach out to him almost as if fearing that her own defences might be breached.

So although they still lived and slept together they found it almost impossible to talk about the boys and share their overwhelming grief with each other and Betty. He had not appreciated how deeply young Betty had taken the loss of her brothers until his two lovely grandsons had arrived. It was when they were to be christened. She wanted Bob to include her brothers in their naming. He, sensible chap, raised no objection, so 'Macdonald' and 'Barry' became their second names.

In retrospect, perhaps it would have helped Jessie, Betty and himself if they had all talked together of their memories at the time instead of bottling them up inside, but they hadn't, and it was too late now. As it was, he used to stand near to the boys, his boys, and talk to them. He recalled that the tears then used to flow more freely and he used to find a comfort and relief in them. He understood so much more, now that they had spoken to him and told him what had happened to them, and how they had died! Oh how that encouraged him to join them and end the torment of this hell on earth.

There were other memories of that ghastly year which came to him. Shortly before Mac's funeral they had been contacted by the Daily Mirror. A young reporter had learnt that they had lost both their sons and apparently wanted to write a short piece about the boys. Jessie had answered the telephone when he had rung Palmers Hill. He, himself, had been at St Cassian's arranging the last details for the service on 4th September.

She said that the reporter had been charming. He had certainly inveigled her into telling him about the letter which Mac had left them. He had rather wished she had kept that private but there it was, she was rightly very proud of Mac, and hadn't. At the reception at the Swan following the funeral Jack Palethorpe had come up to him and shown him the Daily Mirror for that day. There was a short article with pictures of Mac and Barry in uniform. He had read it and remembered it. The article had quoted what Jessie had said.

'My two boys had been staunch pals all their lives. They served in the same squadron together but asked to be parted as they were both worrying that something might happen to them.'

Then there was a short quote from the letter that Mac had written to Jessie.

It was not until 1941 that the headstones had been erected. He and Jessie had been able to select from a small list of Biblical passages which text they wished to appear on each gravestone. Unhesitatingly they had agreed that the inscription should be the same on both graves; that from Isaiah Chapter 40 verse 31 of the

King James Bible, 'They shall mount up with wings as eagles, run and not be weary; walk and not faint.'

The words had run around his brain like a mantra for days after the stones were put in place. Beneath the RAF emblem were the words Flying Officer H. Macd. Goodwin, Pilot, Royal Air Force, Auxiliary Air Force and the date of his death and age 25 then a Christian cross and the inscription below; and on Barry's matching stone his name and rank, Pilot Officer, B. L. Goodwin, Royal Air force, Auxiliary Air Force and the date of his death on 24th June 1940 age 23.

It was not long after the stones had been put in place that he had experienced the odd pins and needles sensation in his feet, and occasions when he felt he was about to lose his balance. He recalled consulting Stephen Gosling about it not at the Surgery in the village but over a whisky at the Lyttelton Arms. Many had been the evenings when he had found solace in whisky there. He had recognised that he had been drinking more heavily than ever before although he recalled he had always had a fair amount to drink. Now though he could not manage without it and he was consuming a bottle a day, sometimes even more. Often he would hide the bottles so that Jessie would not nag him as she frequently did about his alcohol consumption. She would have been horrified had she known its true volume. Anyway Stephen had insisted that he attend the Surgery for some tests.

The tests revealed that he had a condition called neuritis. The tingling in his feet and tremor in his hands were to do with some sort of damage to his peripheral nerves. Stephen had told him to stop drinking straightaway but he had not found that possible. The pain and sensitivity of his feet had year upon year gradually become almost unbearable, and he now lived on a diet of painkillers. He could not bear to have even a light sheet touching the soles of his feet when he was in bed and walking had become a nightmare. Sometimes when he had experienced particularly bad times of it, Stephen had even injected morphine to give him relief. Sleep was often beyond him because of the pain. There was no known cure.

In his youth he had been a good shot with both shotgun and rifle. Indeed, he had competed at Bisley and had come 4th one year in the King's Prize. He still found guns of interest. Sometimes the neuritis was so bad that he simply could not get into work but had lain on his bed most of the day. He recalled wryly how on such a day his grandsons had laughed at him when he had persuaded his gardener to hang targets from trees in the garden at Palmers Hill, but they had been suitably impressed when he had shot them down one by one!

His business once so thriving had faltered as the various pressures took their toll. He had recognised his total lack of interest in it once there was no prospect of working at it to provide for the next generation of Goodwins. His increasing absences through illness and through the neglect that had flowed from his disinterest began to affect the annual turnover and profits. He recalled how his brothers, Stanley and Bernard, had come to speak with him; both of them now successful men in their own right. Stanley's garage business was booming and Bernard was a highly respected hospital consultant and magistrate.

They had obviously been concerned in their own different ways, as to what was happening to his life. They had no appreciation of the seriousness of his illness but spoke as if his grief was the sole problem he had to surmount. They had urged him to pull himself together and make the business work again.

Other families too had lost sons and had moved on. They entreated him to do the same before financial disaster struck. He could not keep Palmers Hill going and continue his lavish lifestyle unless he did. He knew that all their advice was well-intentioned and he had been grateful that the rift with Stanley seemed now so firmly healed. He had tried to respond but found himself almost totally incapable of doing what they had asked.

Family life at Palmers Hill had continued very much to a similar pattern of their shared life with the boys; with weekends spent at Bridewell Cottage, and summer holidays at the Dunes. They no longer travelled abroad now that his neuritis made walking so painful. He supposed that had saved some money but the cost of everything from food to petroleum seemed to be going up and the profits from the business were falling disastrously. The money was running out and he did not think he would be able to sustain the deception for much longer.

He had decided that unless he took drastic action they would not be able to stay at Palmers Hill. The house had become integral to his very existence; a shrine bound up with his memory of the boys; a place where he could sit in their room which was kept totally undisturbed, just as they had left it. He had simply not been able to contemplate losing Palmers Hill while he lived and breathed.

He had gone to see his old friend Cecil Brinton whose advice he had always valued. Cecil had made a few enquiries and as a result he had sold his ailing business for what he regarded as well below its real value, but the deal at least allowed him the status to stay on as a Director with a token salary. Now living almost entirely on that capital, he had managed to maintain the Goodwin lavish lifestyle and no one was the wiser that financially he had terrible problems. But that money had run out faster than he had imagined it ever would.

There was only one solution left to him to preserve their lifestyle. He hated himself for even thinking of it but he was desperate. Nevertheless it had been a dastardly thing to do and had cut him to the quick. He had broken trust with Jessie without her knowing. He had never discussed financial matters with her and she had no inkling at all that they were anything other than financially secure. She would find out soon enough now but he had not been able to bring himself to tell her the truth. He was too ashamed of what he had done to break his secrecy.

A couple of months ago, back in November he had thought he would be able to opt out and make his death look like an accident when Felix had come across from his farm opposite to Palmers Hill to have a drink with him. They had often met to talk across the years and Felix had kindly taken to coming more frequently now that he had virtually stopped going out in the evenings. An accidental shooting would not have led to any Police action against Felix, and would have ensured that his life policies would have been met enabling Jessie to live comfortably afterwards even without having to sell Palmers Hill. Unfortunately, his plan had not worked out.

They had been sitting in his Gun Room. They were talking about guns. He had handed Felix a Smith and Wesson .38 across the desk holding it by its barrel so it was pointing at his chest. Unbeknown to Felix it was loaded and cocked. He had handed it to him in that way, hoping that Felix might catch the trigger as he took it and the gun go off. But Felix had known too much about guns and as he had taken the pistol he had pointed it away and gently lowered the hammer! Felix had asked how to breach the gun. He had been forced to tell him and then Felix had taken the bullets out. Somehow, from the start, he had seen through Laughton's intent for hadn't he said 'Not by my hand old friend!' Shrewd old bugger, Felix. So finally now it had to be him. So many thoughts. So many thoughts.

Chapter 30

ALL IS LOST!

Suddenly, a dry twig snaps on the frosted grass of the glade. Laughton turns towards the sound and sees Jessie walking towards him through the trees looking worried. She is dressed in an old tweed skirt and her patterned brown jumper. He notices that she is still wearing her house slippers. She is shivering in the cold.

'Laughton what are you doing out here? It's so cold and you're still in your dressing gown ...'

Her voice falters as she sees the gun in his hand. He says nothing.

'Laughton my love, I do know. You've never been any good hiding things from me – you know that.'

'What do you know about all these things? You don't understand how it really is for me!'

'But of course I do Laughton, I do! I know we can't pay our debts.'

'How did you find out? I never meant you to have to face this.'

'Robert came to see me. He thought he should warn me.'

'Robert had no right to tell you anything at all. He's my solicitor.'

'No Laughton he had every right. He feared that you would do something stupid like this!'

'This is not stupid. It is the only way out. Palmers Hill; everything we own will have to be sold. Don't you understand there will be nothing left? I have used up all our capital and more! Can you imagine our friends' reaction Jessie? The shame of bankruptcy or worse. I built Palmers Hill for you and the children. It used to ring with their laughter. For a decade now it has been a silent morgue for me. I can live with the silence no longer!'

'What do you mean Laughton 'or worse'?'

Laughton falls silent. He looks down to the ground in front of the bench where he sits still holding the gun.

'What do you mean Laughton 'or worse'?' Jessie repeats.

'Oh Jessie don't ask.'

'No Laughton tell me.'

Another longer silence.

'I forged your signature and sold your Palethorpe shares. They've all been sold.'

140

'No Laughton, oh no!'

'Yes and I am so ashamed. I stole from you Jessie. I stole from my own wife! Let me go Jessie, please let me go!'

Although completely stunned by this revelation Jessie focuses. She must get the gun off Laughton.

'Come on Laughton we have faced worse than this. Look how you came back after the fire. We can come through this. You and me, we are still here!'

'Jessie, don't be ridiculous!' he snorts, 'I was in my thirties then. Now I am a sick old man. I am sixty-eight! Stephen told us there is no cure for my neuritis. I can't come back from this!'

'But at least we would be together. I couldn't bear to be parted from you.'

'Yes, but then you and Betty would have to bear all the shame with me. No Jessie its better this way. It really is!'

'Come on love no one wants this! We'll find a way through just as we always have.' she persists.

He lowers the gun to his side.

'Have we?' he questions.

There is a pause in which neither speaks. Jessie moves to within an arm's length of him but does not touch him.

'Best way out for all of us. But I am such a coward Jessie; I don't know I can do it! Please, please one last kindness I beg you.'

He holds out the gun towards her inviting her acceptance and continues. 'If you really love me, let me go; you're so much stronger than me. You always have been; you finish it. I can't take the black agony any more!'

Tears start again to course down his face and he averts his gaze from her.

Jessie in tears, with a nod of pretence, reaches forward and takes the still loaded gun from his right hand. She must get rid of this gun before he harms himself with it. She takes the gun from his grasp and inside sighs to herself with sheer relief. He will be safe now. Whatever he has done they will get through it; she loves him much too much to lose him now after all these years. She allows herself an inner smile with the relief she now feels.

Now with some purpose, she steps back away from him thinking to throw the gun into the deep undergrowth that surrounds the glade. The heel of one of her slippers catches on a protruding tree root. She trips and falls backwards away from Laughton.

'Crack', the gun fires just once. Laughton looks at her with shock and incredulity, then with the whisper of a smile, as the bullet hits him in the chest near the heart. No pain shows on his face as he collapses to the ground, his life seeping out of him in one last sigh. The smell of cordite lingers.

'Laughton, no! Oh no!' Jessie drops the still smoking gun with a piercing scream 'What have I done? No ......' She falls to Laughton's side. She takes up his head in her arms. It is instantly clear to her that he is beyond help from her or anyone else. Laughton is dead. She is shaking violently with shock, her distraught thoughts absorbed by guilt and grief. Reaching out to her side she picks up the gun. She puts it to her own temple and pulls the trigger!

Author's Epilogue

Until that day in June 2002 Chaddesley Corbett was just another village on the map of Worcestershire. The weather was inclement with squally showers. My wife and I had decided to stay at Brockencote Hall Hotel on the edge of the village. It was our way of celebrating the Queen's Golden Jubilee or some people might say our excuse to get away for the night!

When we arrived and parked only twenty minutes ride from our home in Worcester I felt the need to justify not travelling further and said that I thought we should sit in the car for a while to recover from the journey! As you can see our mood was flippant and neither of us anticipated the discoveries we were to make later that day; discoveries that would have such a profound effect on our lives.

Entering the hotel that had an air of past Victorian splendour, we registered, and parked our bags in our en-suite room before deciding to venture out for a walk in the grounds, simply to get some air. It was, by now, actually raining again so donning our wet gear we set off. Quickly we found that Brockencote Hall did not have any grounds that you can walk in. We soon had explored the small garden and duck pond. So seeing the village of Chaddesley Corbett across the main road we decided that exploration down the drive and across to where we could see a church might be more energetic and rewarding, so off we set.

Five minutes later we were in the village street by the lych-gate of the church where a notice announced that it was St. Cassian's.

'Shall we have a look inside the church?' I asked thinking that at least that would get us out of the rain for a brief time.

'Why not?' Jane countered by way of an answer, she might well have regretted later.

I led the way up the winding path to where I thought the entrance would be at the west end of the church below a square stone crenellated tower. There we found a solid large oak door of some antiquity. I pushed at it only to find it locked and we could not enter. It was Jane who found that the modern day entrance was actually at the side of the tower. The iron handle on that door turned to open it to us. Inside to the right another door led us from the vestibule under the tower, to the nave itself. A typical English village church was revealed obviously lovingly cared for and revered. We could easily see that ancient parts dating back to the 12th Century merged harmoniously with later additions and the smell of recently applied polish on wood permeated.

We spent not much more that a quarter of an hour exploring its various parts and examining its beautiful Norman font; the late 19th Century stained glass above the altar and the brass eagle that adorned the lectern. The Book of Ecclesiasticus from the vulgate was open on its broad wings and I stood on the plinth at its base and read aloud to the empty church the first verses of that wonderful chapter; chapter forty-four, 'Let us now praise famous men and the fathers that begat us; the Lord hath wrought great glory by them through his great power from the beginning......'

Then we walked back towards the door to leave pausing only to make a donation for the upkeep of this beautiful place.

Outside it had stopped raining, and we were about to walk down the path back to the road when I noticed a dripping horse-chestnut tree on the farther side of the graveyard. The wind was moving the boughs to and fro and I just caught a glimpse of something I felt I should look at.

Jane was just closing the outer door to the church.

'I think that there are a couple of Commonwealth War Graves over there. I'm just going over have a look.'

'Oh no,' came the reply, '.........not again!'

This despairing response came because the last such research I had made was into the life of an ordinary 'Tommy' from the First World War whose life had taken fourteen or so years to uncover!

Undeterred by this rather negative response I went over and beneath the heavily leaved branches against the wall of the churchyard there indeed were two white Portland stone marked graves. The two names inscribed were obviously related 'H. Macd. Goodwin' and 'B. L. Goodwin' and the stones revealed that their deaths as young pilots had occurred within weeks of each other in 1940; a time when Britain had been under threat of invasion by Hitler. Were they brothers? Which squadron had they served with? Had they died in the Battle of Britain? How had they died? What a terrible disaster for their family to lose two sons within weeks of each other. My brain buzzed with questions.

I made a note of their details on a scrap of paper and retraced my steps to the Church to find some answers. There were none to be found. There was no mention of these 'boys' anywhere.

We left and went to the local Post Office and asked whether the postmaster knew the 'boys' history. He didn't but told me that the local historical society were having an exhibition of photographs in the Village Hall the following Saturday and perhaps one of the members might be able to help me then. They did and what an extraordinary family story I eventually uncovered; a story of triumphs and disasters which had waited patiently in obscurity for so many years waiting to be discovered and told; the story of Palmers Hill.

Postscript

An Inquest held on Tuesday 25th January 1951 concluded that Laughton Goodwin had taken his own life whilst the balance of his mind was disturbed. Palmers Hill and all its contents were sold by auction on 30th June 1952. Jessie was not present when Laughton took his own life. She later became bedridden and died on 4th December 1953, aged 68. Betty died tragically early in 1960 aged only 39 and her husband, Bob Walker, in 1997. Laughton, Jessie and Betty are all buried near Mac and Barry at St Cassian's Church in Chaddesley Corbett. Betty's two sons, Mike and Tony live on.

Further Reading

We Never Slept – The Story of 605 Squadron – Ian Piper, ISBN 0 9529516 0 6

Fighter Boys – Patrick Bishop [Harper Perennial], ISBN 0 00 653204 7

Under the White Rose – The Story of 609 Squadron – Frank H. Ziegler [MacDonald], ISBN 0 947554 29 7

Brothers in Arms – Chris Goss [Crecy Books], ISBN 0 947554 37 8